VALENTINO

DI SALVO CRIME FAMILY
BOOK FOUR

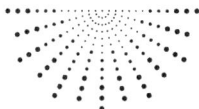

CAMERON HART

WANT A FREE BOOK?

Sign up for my newsletter and get your copy of Chasing Stacy.

River: One look at the stunning waitress carrying the weight of the world on her shoulders, and I'm a gonner. I wasn't looking for a sweet little thing with auburn hair and more baggage than I can fit on the back of my bike, but there's no going back now. She's mine. I'll prove to her I'm more than capable of handling her past and making her feel safe again.

CONNECT WITH ME!

Check out my website, cameronhart.net, for sneak previews on my latest projects.

Follow me on social media:
Facebook Page
Facebook Group
TikTok
Instagram
Goodreads
Bookbub

VALENTINO

I stopped by the abandoned warehouse to check out some suspicious activity that had been reported recently. I thought we had a homeless person or a very stupid thief, but nothing could have prepared me for her. Katya, AKA, the mafia princess of our sworn enemies.

I should kidnap her and hold her for ransom, or possibly send her back to her scheming family with a message for them to back off. Instead, I scoop up the terrified yet determined young woman and tuck her into my bed. I even make hot chocolate for her for some stupid reason.

Katya is the last person I should be getting close to, but every moment in her presence undoes me little by little. I can't get enough of her sassy remarks and sweet kisses.

When my loyalty comes into question, will I be able to prove myself to the Di Salvos and still keep my princess safe?

CHAPTER ONE

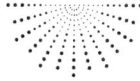

VALENTINO

"*W*hat now?" I grunt over the phone as I unlock my car. Slipping into the driver's seat, I sigh when our newest recruit tells me there's been another break-in by the docks. "And still no idea who it is?"

"No, Captain."

"You don't have to call me captain every time we talk," I tell Michael for the tenth time.

"Yes, Captain."

I roll my eyes but let it go. I remember what it was like starting from nothing in the Di Salvo crime family. In just over ten years, I went from lackey to foot soldier to Capo, charged with maintaining my own territory and commanding my own tier of soldiers. Not only that, but the Boss, Romeo, has trusted me enough to let me into the inner circle.

"Which facility did they hit up this time?" I ask, already frustrated that I'll have to make one last stop before going home for the night. Michael rattles off the address, and I hang up before pulling into New York City traffic.

The drive to the docks isn't horrible, it's just annoying.

For the last three days, my men have been reporting strange things going on around some of our properties. At first, it was petty complaints like missing snacks and lunches throughout the day. Then someone found a makeshift sleeping area in a rarely used storage closet, indicating we had a squatter.

Usually, I'd let someone else handle the riff-raff. This wouldn't be the first time a homeless person thought they found the perfect shelter. After scaring the shit out of them at gunpoint, the protocol is to set them up at one of our cheaper hotels for the night and send them off with an all-you-can-eat continental breakfast in the morning.

Of course, we also let them know if we see them on our property again, we'll shoot first and ask questions later. So far, no one has come back.

Everyone in the family is on high alert right now, however, this situation needs a more delicate touch. While I'm nearly one hundred percent certain it's another squatter, there's a small chance the Colombos, our rivals, are trying some shit again.

We know war is on the horizon, which means every detail matters. Including riff-raff.

I turn my headlights off before pulling into the alley leading to the warehouse in question. Parking in the shadows next to the building, I make sure I have my gun at my side and my knife secured to my ankle before stepping out and heading inside.

I debate whether or not to turn on the lights and scare the shit out of whoever is trying to sneak around, but ultimately decide to go the stealthy route. Grabbing a flashlight from the bench inside the door, I proceed to walk around the perimeter of the open room, shining the light into all the little hiding spots where someone could be lurking.

A macabre sense of power settles over me. I know it's

fucked up, but I enjoy these kinds of missions. For so long, I was the one who hid from monsters. Now, here I am, the monster other people run in fear from.

I suppose a sinister outlook on life is required for a made man such as myself. I don't mind. I've worked my ass off to get to where I am today, and if my dark, twisted heart helped pave the way, so be it.

A muffled sound catches my attention, and I freeze, waiting to hear it again. Silence stretches on for long moments, and I almost think I imagined it, but then I hear it again. Clearer this time.

A sneeze.

"Gotcha," I say under my breath as I stride toward the corner where the noise came from.

There's nowhere for the trespasser to go. Pallets filled with contraband to be sold are stacked fifteen feet high on one side, and on the other, a wide-open area leading to a locked and reinforced steel door. If they run, I'll sink a bullet into them long before they're able to escape.

Moving in closer, I see a few empty pallets leaning up against the wall at an angle, creating a makeshift barrier. I probably wouldn't have noticed it if not for the sneeze that drew me to this spot.

I creep along the side, keeping my flashlight pointed away until I get to the shadowed entrance. Then, all at once, I flash the bright, powerful light on the intruder and point my gun right between their eyes.

Round, golden irises blink up at me, catching me off-guard. It takes a second for my vision to adjust to the harsh light, but when I see the woman huddled on the ground with her legs tucked up and her arms around her knees, I feel like I might collapse. In fact, my knees shake, forcing me to squat down before toppling over.

What the fuck is happening to me?

I keep my gun trained on the woman, but I can't keep my eyes from wandering over her face, taking in her delicate features. Midnight black hair frames her large eyes and round cheeks, and her nose is slightly curved at the end, giving her a doll-like appearance.

Well, shit. I've never encountered a sweet little thing like her in a dark and dangerous place like this. It's usually delusional old drunks or meth addicts. I can tell by the clarity in her eyes she's not under the influence of drugs or alcohol, which only makes her presence here that much more puzzling.

"I-I'll come out," she says, her voice scratchy and barely above a whisper. "Please don't hurt me."

Jesus, why does my chest feel like it's caving in on itself at her words? I should be happy. This is going to be easier than I thought.

I grunt, lowering my weapon and nodding once. I'm about to stand from my position when the mysterious woman screeches and lunges at me, tackling me to the floor before scrambling off.

I jerk to the side and jump to my feet, cursing when I see my gun a few feet away from me on the ground.

"Don't even think about it," the woman says, causing me to whip my head in her direction.

She has a goddamn Glock pointed at me, and I'm not sure whether to be furious that she outsmarted me or impressed that this five-foot-nothing trespasser has me dead to rights within seconds of meeting me. Not many people can say they've gotten the drop on me. Actually, no one has, that I can remember.

I raise my hands, palms out, in surrender, as I take stock of my new situation. My gun is out of reach. My knife is on me, but I can't get to it without risking a bullet to the brain. Training my gaze on the threat, I notice the gun is shaking.

The woman is shaking, too. Trembling, in fact, from head to toe.

Her eyes tell a different story. I see a fierce look I recognize all too well; the animalistic need to survive. A golden flame flickers in her irises, a warning to anyone that her light won't easily be extinguished.

I have no idea who the hell this woman is, though the more I look at her, the more familiar she seems. Still, I know she's seen some shit. She's fought for her life from the moment she was born, and she managed to claw her way out, only to come face to face with a mafia captain and his gun. She's the exact kind of wild card with nothing to lose that I was at her age.

Maybe that's why I feel this inexplicable connection to her. She's young and terrified and angry at the world, and some part of me has the crazy urge to be the one person she can trust.

I take a step forward, my hands still up in surrender, and the woman shoves her weapon further toward me, though it slips from her sweaty grip slightly.

"You're going to hurt yourself more than me with that thing," I tell her, playing everything off like it's no big deal. She's desperate to project confidence and control, so letting her know I'm not phased is key.

"Bold, for someone with a gun pointed at their head," she quips. I'll give her credit, her voice is steady and full of venom.

"I hate to break it to you, princess, but this isn't the first time I've had a weapon drawn on me."

Her face turns pale, those round eyes growing impossibly bigger at something I said. "How did you…?"

I take advantage of her apparent confusion and move a few steps closer. "How did I what?" I ask smoothly.

"H-how did you know who I am?"

I raise an eyebrow and give her an enigmatic smile, not wanting to give away that I have no idea what she's talking about. I wish I knew who she was. The woman looks familiar and exotic at the same time. It's something to do with her eyes…

Princess.

The word pops into my head. I called her princess. I have no idea why I did that. It just came out of my mouth. Is that what she means? Her name is Princess?

Oh, fuck.

It hits me like a lead pipe to the sternum. Princess isn't her name, it's her *position.*

Katya Colombo, daughter of Marco Colombo, the head of the rival family we're on the brink of war with. She's a mafia princess. A sheltered one at that, presumably to keep prying eyes off her. There's no way this coddled woman knows how to load and shoot a gun.

In one swift and calculated move, I snag the weapon from her trembling hand, sliding it across the concrete floor a good hundred feet away or so. Grabbing my own piece from where she knocked it out of my hand, I point it at her, turning the tables once more.

"What the fuck are you doing here, Katya?" I spit out. I can't believe I felt sorry for her, though I shouldn't be surprised. Every woman I've ever known is only out for their own interests. They'll lie, cheat, steal, and manipulate anyone and everyone to further their agenda. Of course, Katya is no different.

"Not what you think," she answers, standing her ground.

She knows I won't kill her. Not yet, at least. Katya could be an important player in our war.

"Doesn't matter much what I think," I scoff. "But the Boss will be interested to know who our little trespasser is. Maybe we'll hold you for ransom or send you back with a message," I muse, though the words sound hollow to my ears.

Each one physically pains me, though I can't for the life of me understand why. She's the enemy. She's leverage. I shouldn't care about her safety, and I certainly shouldn't hesitate to call Romeo and tell him who I found.

And yet, I know deep down that I don't want anyone else to know. I don't want anyone else to touch her. Fuck me, these possessive feelings over another human are intense and unwelcome, and I'm not sure what to do about them.

"If you send me back to my family, I better be in a body bag," Katya says with a surprising amount of conviction. "I'm done with them. I want nothing to do with their plans, their wars, their agendas. I'm done being a pawn. So if you want to send a message, by all means, go for it. Sending my father my head on a platter would do the trick."

Katya further shocks me by spreading her arms out as if bracing for an execution shot. That's when I see blood soaking through her shirt, on her left side, right about where her ribs are.

The air drains from my lungs so quickly I grow light-headed. An unfamiliar sensation strikes at my core like a flash of lightning, electrocuting every nerve as I watch the red stain grow larger.

Fuck. Did I hurt her?

Panic courses through me as I lower my gun, followed quickly by guilt. Two things I haven't allowed myself to acknowledge since leaving home at eighteen.

"You're bleeding," I grit out, still confused as to why the thought of Katya in pain makes me angry.

"It's fine," she's quick to supply. "I patched it up a few days ago."

I grind my teeth together, my jaw tense as my nostrils flare. She's been wounded for days, and it clearly hasn't been properly tended to. She could get it infected if it isn't already.

Another thought rears its ugly head, just as confusing as the previous ones.

Who the fuck made her bleed in the first place? I'll do the same to them before ending their miserable life.

Jesus, I need to get it together.

"Not very well," I say, nodding to the blood on her shirt.

Katya looks down, wincing when she sees the stain. "Fuck," she says to herself, her hand instinctively coming up to cover the spot.

Her face contorts in pain, but she doesn't make a sound. I try not to let that bother me, but it doesn't sit right. How many times has she silently screamed, praying for someone to somehow hear her cries?

I shake my head of those thoughts, not liking the road they were taking me down. "You need stitches," I state.

"No," comes the automatic response.

"It's going to get infected."

"If I'm about to die, does it really matter?"

"We both know I'm not going to kill you."

Katya narrows her eyes at me, tearing me apart piece by piece. I'm not sure what she sees, but for the first time in my life, I worry about measuring up. Ridiculous, I know.

"Still. I'm not going to a hospital, and I sure as hell don't trust a Di Salvo doctor."

"Fair enough," I say with a nod. She's right, neither one of those options is a good one. For either of us. "I have an extensive first aid kit in my home. I'll take you there and stitch you up."

"Pass."

"Then I'll just take you to Romeo as is, I guess."

Katya glares at me, her jaw clenched and chin jutted out in defiance. I know that look, too. She's cornered. Trapped.

Forced to decide between two shitty outcomes. She doesn't know, however, that there's no way in hell I'm taking this injured, terrified woman straight to the lion's den. Fuck if I can explain why, I just know I need to get her to my place, where she'll be safe.

"Fine," Katya concedes, her shoulders drooping slightly.

"Good. Now, follow me out to my car, and don't try anything stupid." I try to sound like the gruff, no-nonsense Capo I am, but with Katya, everything comes out a little softer. I hate it.

"Can I at least know the name of my captor?" she mumbles, eyeing me warily.

"Valentino," I clip out.

Katya barely makes it three steps before doubling over, clutching her side as she hisses. I'm next to her in an instant, and before I even realize what's happening, she's in my arms, cradled against me. I ignore the feeling of something settling deep in my chest now that she's in my care.

"I'm fine," Katya whimpers, though I can feel her muscles jerking in pain with every step I take.

Why is it excruciating to see her suffer like this? I want to absorb her trauma, whatever it may be, and make it my own so she never has to feel this way again.

I'm fucking losing it.

We make it out to my car, where I carefully set her down, though I keep an arm around her waist. Opening the passenger door, I guide Katya to sit before taking off my suit jacket. She gives me a questioning look as I fold it up and hand it to her.

"Press it over the wound to help stop the bleeding," I tell her, nodding as she does what I say.

Katya makes a tiny sound of pain in the back of her throat, and my heart twists inside my chest, wanting to break free and comfort her. I grunt at my obsessive thoughts, then fasten Katya's seatbelt, careful to avoid her left side.

Climbing into the driver's seat, I start the car and slowly exit the gravel lot, trying to avoid the major potholes so as not to jostle Katya too much. Looking over at the confounding woman, my chest grows tight once more. Her eyes are squeezed shut, and her shoulders are hunched up to her ears as she holds my jacket against her side.

I have no clue what the fuck I got myself into, only that I need to patch this woman up and find out more of her story. Then I'll know what to do with her.

CHAPTER TWO

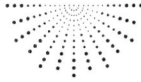

KATYA

*W*ell, this didn't go as planned.

Not that I had much of a plan when I was climbing through my third-story window at midnight three days ago. Still, I didn't think I'd find myself bleeding out in a car with a Di Salvo next to me, supposedly driving me to safety. I'll believe it when I see it.

The car hits a bump and I bite my lip to silence the scream fighting its way out. My left side burns as the stiff fabric rubs against my exposed wound, but I do my best to think of something else. Anything else.

Like how the last thing I ate was a stale, snack-sized bag of goldfish I found, and my stomach feels like it's dissolving into itself with hunger. Or the massive headache that's been residing behind my eyes for the last twenty-four hours. Could be from hunger, stress, illness, lack of sleep, or with any luck, a giant tumor that will render me unconscious soon. That has to be a better death than whatever the Di Salvos have in mind for me.

"Keep pressure on it," Valentino snaps, momentarily taking his eyes off the road to glare at me.

"Worried about me bleeding all over your leather seats?" I quip.

"No."

I raise my eyebrows in surprise, but the man doesn't elaborate any further. Surely he's not worried about *me*, so I'm confused why he cares.

The car in front of us honks, then slams on its breaks, causing Valentino to do the same. The seatbelt digs into my left side, right over the cut on my ribs. It feels like my skin is being flayed off one centimeter at a time, and I can't help the pathetic cry torn from my lips.

"Jesus Christ," Valentino curses.

At first, I think he's upset with me for making a scene. My father would be. But then Valentino's brown eyes rest on mine, and I'm left breathless at the concern I find in them. He looks angry, but this time, it's not directed at me. It seems to be directed at whatever or whoever hurt me.

His large hand covers mine, and together, we hold his jacket against my side.

"Who did this to you? One of my men?"

I blink up at him, still in shock. He looks like he's about to call every single mafia soldier he knows and line them up at gunpoint until someone confesses. That can't be right, though. This man has no reason to be protective of me.

"No."

He grunts in frustration, which I enjoy a little too much. Knowing nothing of Valentino aside from what little time we've spent together, I sense he's someone who always has an answer for everything. I also get the feeling he's used to getting answers from others as well, which must make me extra irritating to him.

"We're almost there," Valentino informs me, changing the subject.

A few moments later, we pull into a gorgeous home

tucked away on a decent-sized estate. The landscaping is flawless, and I find myself gaping at the trees and lush greenery as we wind our way up the long drive.

Valentino parks and jumps out of the car, hardly giving me time to take a breath before he opens my door. I swing my legs out and stand, only to be immediately scooped up in Valentino's arms. My body instinctively curls up against his, and despite knowing better, I cling to the massive man currently cradling me in his embrace. For just a moment, I soak up the strength and power emanating from him, letting myself feel safe and cared for.

When we get inside, the confusing man sets me down on his table. I make a move to jump down, but he gives me a stern look that has me feeling all sorts of unfamiliar emotions. Why does he have to be so... sexy?

Ugh, it's so dumb that I'm even aware of his looks, but it's hard not to notice when he's a foot taller than me, rippling with lean muscle, covered in ink, and giving me possessive glances with his deep brown eyes. It doesn't help that his nose and cheekbones are perfectly angled or that the slight stubble on his jaw makes him look impossibly gruff and refined at the same time.

"Here," he says, handing me a mug. I was too lost in my silly fantasy to notice Valentino grabbed a few things from the kitchen, including a first aid kit.

I take the mug, scrunching up my nose when I see the tiny amount of amber liquid inside.

"What is it?"

"Bourbon," he answers before taking a swig straight from the bottle. "You'll need it."

"I'm not old enough yet," I say for some stupid reason.

Valentino freezes, then slowly sets the bottle down. "How old are you, Katya?" he asks, his voice deeper than before.

"Twenty."

Something like relief spreads over his face, though he schools his features quickly. Weird.

"Close enough," he states, nodding to the mug in my hand.

"Not comforting words coming from the man who's about to give me stitches," I grumble. I swear I see the barest spark of amusement in his eyes, but it's gone before I can be sure.

I hold my breath and take the shot, frowning as the liquid burns its way down my throat and into my stomach.

"Good. Now lie back and lift your shirt." I balk at him, but he rolls his eyes. "Don't be weird about it. Just lift the hem enough to show me the wound."

I do as he says, resting my back against the cool tabletop and inching my shirt up. The cut is only a few inches below my bra line, and I hesitate slightly before taking the whole damn shirt off. Didn't think the first time someone saw me in my bra would be like this, but hey. For girls like me who come from families like mine, it's not the worst way for it to happen.

"Jesus," Valentino hisses, sitting down on a nearby chair and scooting it closer. He leans forward on the table, hovering his fingers above the three-inch cut. "What happened? Who did this to you?" he asks again.

"Does it matter?"

Valentino frowns at me but takes the hint. He gets to work disinfecting the wound, which isn't so bad. At least this pain is productive. When he presses on the wound and pushes my skin back together, however, I howl in pain.

"It's okay," he soothes.

"Easy for you to say," I grit out.

"It's not as bad as I thought. You'll just need some butterfly bandages and antibiotic cream."

"Told you I had it handled."

"You didn't let me finish," he scolds, returning his attention to my side. "It's not as bad as I thought, but left alone any longer, you'd risk infection. And a nasty scar."

"Wouldn't be the first one, doc."

He pauses, taking a second to let my response sink in. I don't know why I told him that. Thankfully, Valentino doesn't say anything.

"I'm not a doctor," he informs me as he takes out several small butterfly bandages and lines them up on the table. "But I learned how to take care of injuries at a young age. I had a lot of practice over the years on myself and my mom."

His confession is as heartbreaking as it is surprising. Valentino looks shocked and slightly embarrassed at what he just said.

Without thinking, I rest my hand over his, squeezing gently. "I'm so sorry," I whisper, meaning every word.

I understand more than he knows, and I hate he had to go through that. No one deserves to be treated that way, and I can't imagine being the kid in that situation, having to take care of your parent.

"I didn't mean to tell you that," he says, sounding flustered.

"It's not like my family is much better. I mean, you've met some of them, I assume."

This earns me a snort, which I'm considering a win. I wonder if Valentino ever smiles, or furthermore if he ever laughs. I have the sudden need to hear it. I bet it's contagious.

"Tell me what happened," he commands more than asks. "I told you something about me, it's only fair you do the same."

I glare at him right as he pinches my cut and secures it with the first butterfly bandage. I hiss and pound the table with my fist but manage not to whimper.

"It'll distract you from the pain," Valentino adds.

"Doubt it," I breathe, preparing for another pinch.

"Try," he tells me before repeating the process with a second bandage.

"My dad's business associate," I blurt out, hoping it covers up the cry of pain. "I met him for the first time four days ago." Valentino nods, encouraging me to continue as he works on my side. "My father called me into his office and told me to introduce myself to my new husband."

Valentino growls, his brown eyes fierce with something I can't quite make out. "Then what?" he rasps, focusing his attention on the next bandage.

"He said…" I bite my bottom lip, not wanting to relive the incident but knowing I have no choice. "He said he wanted to sample the goods," I murmur. "My dad was right there. Sitting in the corner," I say with more conviction. "He watched Raffe grab me and just… just sat there."

"Fucking bastard," Valentino snarls. "Did he… fuck, princess. I don't know how to ask this." Brown eyes meet mine, pleading with me to tell him the truth.

No one has ever cared this much about me, and it's perplexing and overwhelming to think it's coming from my family's sworn enemies.

"I didn't let him touch me," I whisper. "Not like that."

"Thank fuck," he says softly, true relief flooding his eyes. As if the rest of my statement is just catching up to him, Valentino's eyes turn from reassured to pure rage. "How did he touch you, then?"

I wave my hand over my side, showcasing the answer. "He wrapped his hand around my neck and tossed me into a side table. I broke a lamp and landed right on the biggest shard of ceramic."

"And your father just let it happen?" he asks as he places a large Band-Aid over the four butterfly bandages holding my cut together. Valentino helps me sit up, then takes a seat in his chair, his eyes locked on mine and waiting for an answer.

"He was concerned when I fell, but only because visible scars are unacceptable. If I cut my face, he probably would have sent me to a plastic surgeon."

"How can he just... Damnit," he grunts, taking a deep breath. "That's insane, Katya."

Indignation spikes my heart rate as it flows through my veins. "You seriously don't believe me?" I spit out. "I didn't even want to tell you in the first place, and now you're calling me crazy? How–"

"I believe you," Valentino says, cutting me off. He holds my gaze, those deep brown eyes lulling me into a sense of safety, almost against my will. "I believe you, Katya," he says again, his hand resting on my hip. I'm all too aware I'm only in my bra and pants, but there's nothing I can do about it now. The rough pad of his thumb caresses my bare skin in a calming gesture, and it feels far too good. I'm not sure he's even aware he's doing it. "I'm sorry you had to experience that."

For the tenth time today, I'm left speechless and bewildered by this man. He's apologizing for my pain?

Tears rush to the surface, and I try blinking them away before they drown me completely. I can't do this right now. I can't break down in front of Valentino. I can't feel these emotions, can't accept his kindness, can't do anything but force it all down and pretend nothing bothers me like I always do.

Only it's not working this time.

My teeth chatter as my eyes fill with tears, but still, Valentino never looks away. Slowly, so slowly, he lifts his hand toward my face, giving me plenty of time to back away. I don't want to, though. I'm desperate for more of his attention, more of his surprisingly tender touch.

Valentino cups my cheek, brushing away the first tear as it falls. "You're safe here," he murmurs.

I shake my head no, unable to believe him, even if I want to. "For how long?"

Something dark flashes across his eyes, followed quickly by a practiced look of indifference. I recognize it all too well. Valentino drops his hand from my cheek and stands, taking a step back as if being close to me is now dangerous.

"I'll check on the wound in the morning and change the Band-Aid," he says matter-of-factly.

He's back to being cold and business-like, which is probably for the best. We both shared some shit in the heat of the moment, but it's wiser to shut up and keep our distance.

"I won't be here in the morning," I point out, gingerly climbing down from the table. I ignore Valentino's hand as he reaches out to help.

"Of course, you will. You'll be staying here tonight. Your room is the second door on the left."

"Excuse me?" I question. I gather up my bloody shirt from the table, not wanting to put it back on but also not wanting to be this exposed. I ball the fabric up and hold it in front of my chest, attempting to cover as much skin as possible.

"Oh, did you have other plans tonight? Another warehouse with better accommodations, maybe?"

I narrow my eyes at the enigmatic man, who is vulnerable one minute and aloof the next.

"Fine," I concede. He's right. I have nowhere else to go.

"It's settled then. Bathroom is across the hall. Don't get your bandage wet, but you can clean up. I'll put some clothes outside."

I nod as my stomach lets out an embarrassing growl. Valentino stares at me, then drops his eyes to my belly, which I instinctively cover up.

"Dinner will be waiting for you in the microwave. Heat it

up when you're ready. I'll be retiring to my room for the night."

Without another word, he spins on his heel and stomps upstairs.

"I'll be retiring to my room for the night," I mimic under my breath in a mocking voice. Who says stuff like that?

I wait around the kitchen for a few moments, taking a look at the stainless-steel appliances and marble countertops. I want to give him plenty of time to brood before he *retires* for the night.

Despite the whiplash of emotions from Valentino, I feel… safe here. Just like he promised. Good things don't last, and I'm not expecting this to, either. I'll take advantage of the shower and warm bed for the night and be on my way tomorrow morning.

I'm sure I'll have figured out my next move by then.

CHAPTER THREE

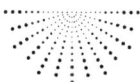

VALENTINO

"*D*o you have an update on who's been sneaking around the docks?" Romeo asks over the phone.

Shit.

I pace from one side of my living room to the other, racking my brain for something to say. Why didn't I think about coming up with something before our call?

I know the answer before I'm even finished asking myself the question. I never thought I'd lie to the Boss. For the last fourteen years, my only goal has been to make him proud to have me in the family. When Romeo let me into his inner circle, I swore to myself I would never do anything to jeopardize my position in the family.

And then Katya burst into my life, quite literally, and everything I thought I valued was turned upside down. Without even realizing it, the little princess sleeping upstairs has become my new obsession.

So much so, I'm about to break the one rule I never thought I would.

"Valentino? I'm a busy man with three more calls to make this evening."

"Yes. Sorry, Boss. It was nothing to be alarmed about," I tell him, each word tasting like betrayal. "Someone was just hiding out from a bad situation." At least that's not a *total* lie.

Yeah, whatever helps you sleep at night, my brain unhelpfully adds.

"And you took care of it? Regular protocol?"

"Yes," I force out, gritting my teeth.

Romeo is silent for long moments, and I'm sure he's about to tell me I'm a fucking liar and strip me of my position, hell, even exile me completely. Except men like me, men at the top who know sensitive information, don't get exiled. We get executed.

My heart hammers away in my chest, though I manage to control my breathing. I've gotten quite talented at shutting down any emotion, including fear.

"Good," Romeo finally says. The panic clawing its way up my throat slowly recedes. "That's good to hear. I was concerned it was a fucking Colombo goon."

"Nope. Definitely not a goon." Another partial truth that does little to allay my guilt.

"Good," he states again, sounding a bit distracted. He's already moving on to the next phone call he needs to make, so we say our goodbyes.

I let out a relieved breath once he hangs up.

"Fuck me," I mutter under my breath.

What the hell am I going to do about Katya? I can't seem to let her go. Any outcome other than staying under my protection is unacceptable. No way in hell am I sending her back to her piece of shit father and the degenerate man he promised her to.

I also can't bring her in front of Romeo, not only because he'd know I was lying, but also because I don't want her to be a pawn in this war. She's been objectified and manipulated her entire life to be whatever her father wants. I can't explain

21

it, but I'd rather take a sucker punch with brass knuckles than put Katya in a situation like that ever again.

A soft noise catches my attention, and I look in the direction of the stairs. Before I have a chance to comprehend what it might be, a guttural scream slices through the silence, striking me to my very core.

I bolt up the stairs two at a time, picking up my pace when I hear another agonizing cry from Katya's room. Without hesitation, I fling the door open, not sure how to comprehend what's happening.

She's thrashing around on the bed, her eyes squeezed shut even as tears stain her cheeks. "I'm sorry," she pleads, her voice scratchy from crying and yelling.

I approach the bed with caution, not wanting to scare her, but needing to fix this, to protect her, even from the nightmares in her own head.

"Katya," I say soothingly, climbing onto the bed with her. Her hair is matted down with sweat, her face blotchy and twisted in pain. "You're safe, princess. It's just a dream."

I try holding her hand to comfort her, but she shrinks away from my touch. Jesus, it hurts to see her afraid of me, but I know it's not intentional. Whatever dream she's having has swallowed her whole.

She jerks to the side, and that's when I see a blood stain on the shirt of mine she's wearing.

"Dammit," I rasp. She ripped her bandage off during all of this. I need to stop her before she hurts herself anymore.

I move closer to the terrified woman, then gather her tense body up in my arms, holding her against my chest. Jesus, she's trembling, and fear radiates off her in waves.

"Kayta, wake up," I whisper. "Wake up. It's not real."

She furrows her brows, and her movements become less jerky.

"You're safe," I continue, talking to her in soft, calming

tones. "I'm right here. I'll protect you from the whole goddamn world."

Katya stills in my arms, then opens her eyes, which are filled with confusion. "Wh-what happened?" she murmurs, sounding strained. "Oh, my god. Did I have a nightmare?" she whispers as her confusion gives way to shame.

I hate seeing her like this. I nod, not loosening my hold on her. She doesn't make a move to get out of my arms, so I keep her close. "It's nothing to be ashamed of, princess."

"It's a weakness," she all but whispers. "Other people can just, I don't know. They can just shove everything into a dark corner of their mind and lock it away. All the pain, all the memories, every scar, every lie. They just push all the trauma to the side and somehow move on. I've tried. God, I've tried. But at night…"

"All the monsters come out of that dark corner in your mind," I finish for her.

Katya hits me with her golden eyes, a heartbreaking look etched on her features. Without words, I know what she's thinking. She feels seen and understood for the first time in her life.

She nods, more tears gathering in her eyes. "Yeah," she says with a sniffle, adjusting herself to a more seated position in my lap.

I tuck some of her inky black hair behind her ears, moving slowly so I don't startle her. Cupping her cheek like I did yesterday, I wipe away her tears with the pad of my thumb. Her skin is silky smooth, and Katya tugs at my already shattered heart when she leans into my touch, nuzzling against the palm of my hand.

I guide her to rest against my shoulder, and she does, curling up and tucking her head in between my neck and shoulder. Combing my fingers through Katya's long hair, I hold her close, just letting my presence be enough

Her quiet sniffles turn into sobs as she fists my shirt, her tears wetting my skin. I gently cup the back of her neck, keeping her close while stroking her back with my other hand. I have her all wrapped up so nothing can hurt her ever again.

"I-I can't," she chokes out.

"Can't what, baby?" I'm not sure where the term of endearment came from, but it fits.

"Can't cry," comes her muffled response.

"I don't know, you seem to be doing a good job of it right now," I tease.

Katya pops her head up from where it was buried in the side of my neck, glaring at me with her gorgeous eyes. "I didn't mean I couldn't *physically* cry," she says, narrowing her eyes even more. "I just meant…" Katya trails off, looking over my shoulder instead of meeting my gaze. "I mean, I can't handle it all crashing down. If I feel one thing, I have to feel them all, and, and, and… I can't. I just can't."

Her confession resonates with something deep inside me, and at this moment, it's just Katya and me, connecting on a level that's excruciatingly raw yet healing at the same time.

"The only way out of the fear is through," I whisper. "You can't avoid the bad, scary, and devastating things that happen to you. Not unless you want those memories to jump out and pull you under when you're most vulnerable."

"Like in my sleep?"

I nod. "Like in your sleep."

Katya takes a deep breath and exhales slowly, her muscles finally drained of the last of their tension. "And talking about it will help?" Again, I nod. "Well, shit."

This startles a laugh out of me. Katya's face instantly lights up, the most adorable smile gracing her lips. What did I do to earn such a precious gift?

"I like your laugh," she says, her eyes twinkling as she beams up at me.

It's not often I'm at a loss for words. Right now, however, I've got nothing.

"I need to change your bandage," I say, changing the subject before I do something stupid like kiss her and tell her to stay with me forever.

Katya's smile drops as she looks down at her side. "Sorry," she murmurs, holding her hand over the blood stain as though that would make it disappear.

It kills me that she's apologizing for her pain. It speaks volumes about what she's been through in her short life.

"Nothing to be sorry about, Katya," I tell her softly. "You did nothing wrong."

Golden eyes blink up at me in confusion and disbelief, but beneath the layers of insecurities and distrust, I see a tentative hope. I want to bring that out in her, to give her hope and joy and all the other shit I never thought I cared about. I may not deserve any of it, but Katya does. She deserves every good thing in this world, and for some reason I still can't comprehend, I need to be the one to give it to her.

"None of this is your fault," I whisper, running my finger-tips up and down her arm in a calming gesture. "Now, let's get you cleaned up and back to bed, yeah?"

Katya nods, her eyes never leaving mine. It's intense, the way she looks at me. Like she's burrowing down into my very soul and making space for herself. She doesn't need to try so hard. I already know I'll never forget this woman.

I help her off the bed and half-carry her to the bathroom across the hall, sitting her down on the edge of the tub. After grabbing the first aid kit from the drawer next to the sink, I kneel down in front of Katya and begin to lift the hem of her shirt.

She immediately crosses her arms over her chest, and I

look up, lifting an eyebrow in question. "I have to see it so I know how to patch you up."

"I know, I just…" She trails off, looking to the side to avoid my gaze. Finally, Katya sighs and drops her arms to her sides. "I'm not wearing a bra," she whispers.

"Oh." At first, I'm not sure why that information is relevant. I didn't think about it, but it makes sense that she wouldn't sleep in a bra. "*Oh*," I say again once I realize what the issue is. She has to take off her shirt for me to have access, which means…

"It's fine, I mean, I know it's not a big deal," she rushes to say, her cheeks glowing red. "I just haven't ever shown anyone… I mean, it's not like I've even had… Oh my *god*, never mind." Katya finishes her outburst by covering her face with her hands.

What the hell just happened? What is she talking about?

Then it hits me. More like bludgeons me. *I've never shown anyone… I've never even had…*

Jesus. This woman is killing me. Never thought I had a possessive bone in my body until now, but hearing her admit she's never been with anyone? No one has touched her, kissed her, seen her naked curves…

"It's okay," I manage to say, hopefully not sounding as feral as I feel. "Nothing to be ashamed of." *In fact, I love it. More than I should.* "I'll turn around while you take the shirt off. You can, uh, cover what you need to cover as long as I have access to the cut."

I turn, giving her my back so she can undress in private. I'd much rather insist she goes topless, but no way in hell will I ever pressure her or disrespect her boundaries. This girl has had enough people trample all over her wants and needs, and I refuse to be another one.

"Valentino?" comes her soft voice. "I, um, I need help with the shirt. I think some of the blood dried, and… I trust you."

The last part is barely above a whisper, but I hear it as if it were a gunshot next to my ear. *She trusts me.*

I grab a washcloth and dampen it slightly before turning to face Katya. She's nibbling on her bottom lip, looking up at me with those wide, vulnerable eyes. Without saying a word, I gently press the damp cloth to her side, loosening the dried blood so it releases the bond between her skin and the fabric.

Tugging on the shirt slightly, I manage to lift it off of the wound fairly easily, thank God. I hate the thought of putting her through any more pain. Curling my fingers under the hem of the shirt, I slowly lift the fabric up, up, up her body, revealing creamy skin and round, firm breasts I don't allow myself to stare at.

Once the shirt is over her head, Katya captures my eyes. She's stunning but now isn't the time.

"You're beautiful, Katya," I find myself saying. "Now, let's get you cleaned up and back to bed."

I kneel once more, focusing all of my attention on cleaning her wound. Luckily, none of the butterfly bandages ripped off, just the large Band-Aid covering everything up. The skin around the cut is red, but the wound itself is actually healing up better than I hoped. With another few days of rest, it'll close and heal on its own.

For now, I put on another layer of antibiotic cream to help speed the process along. After covering the area with another bandage, I lightly trace my fingertips along the outside to make sure everything is secure.

Looking up at Katya, she gives me a tiny smile that lights up my world.

"I'll be right back," I tell her, dashing to my room to grab another shirt. "Here." I hold the shirt open above her head, and she understands, lifting her arms so I can slide the shirt over her gorgeous body.

"Thank you," she murmurs, tucking a few strands of hair

behind her ear. "For everything. I don't know what would have happened if someone else found me."

I grit my teeth, not liking the thought of that one bit. If it were someone else, she would be in a world of trouble.

"You're here now, that's all that matters." Another small smile graces her lips. I want to taste it, but that's so far beyond inappropriate for so many reasons. "Can I help you back to bed? Or do you want some water? A snack?"

Her head perks up, those damn eyes sparkling in a way that makes my chest tight. "Do you have hot chocolate?"

"Do I look like someone who has hot chocolate on hand?"

This earns me a quiet laugh and a shake of her head. "No, I suppose not," she says with a smile. "I'll be fine. Thank you again."

I don't know what to say to her, so I just offer my hand. She stands, and I lead her across the hall to her room, peeling back the covers so she can climb in. Once settled, I cover her with the blankets, tucking in the precious, strong, gorgeous princess.

I'm about to leave her when the question that's been burning in my mind all night comes spilling out without my permission.

"What was your nightmare about?"

Katya's eyes dim as she curls in on herself.

"Most of the time, it's flashes of conversations I've had with my father. His biting words take physical form and litter my skin with bruises. Sometimes he leaves me to bleed out in his office. Sometimes he carries my body to the river and tosses me in. Tonight…" She trails off, squeezing her eyes shut. "Tonight, he shot me in the face."

"Katya," I whisper, my hand finding hers beneath the blankets. "I will never let that happen," I vow.

"But how–"

"Never," I repeat. "You said you trusted me earlier. Is that still true?" She nods her head. "Then get some rest, princess."

I'm rewarded by a shy smile, that blush creeping into her cheeks once more. Only this time, I hope it's because she feels cared for and not ashamed.

"Goodnight, Valentino."

"Goodnight, Katya."

I step out of her room and shut the door, leaning against it.

What the fuck am I going to do now?

CHAPTER FOUR

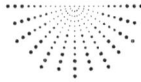

KATYA

I've been awake for a while now, but I can't bring myself to get out of bed. Not yet. It's so soft and warm, and after three nights of sleeping on cement floors and hiding in crates, this mattress feels heavenly.

Rolling onto my back, memories of last night slowly rise to the surface. I was sound asleep, more at peace than I can ever remember, and then…

Oh, God. I had a nightmare.

Every muscle in my body tenses as the horrifying image of my father pulling a gun on me flashes across my mind. I remember crying out for someone, anyone, to help. It's never worked before, but this time, Valentino answered my call.

I cover my face with my hands, the embarrassment of being weak in front of Valentino too much to bear. He didn't make me feel fragile or silly for having a nightmare. In fact, the puzzling man held me in his arms and whispered surprisingly sweet things to me until I could breathe again.

More moments from our interaction last night bubble up, each one more vulnerable than the last. Valentino saw more of me than any man ever has, and what's more, he called me *beautiful.* Me. I don't think anyone has ever said that to me. Certainly not my parents.

My father never spared me a glance unless I could be a useful pawn in his latest scheme. His compliments always came with a bite. *Your dress is lovely. It would be even better if you dropped twenty pounds.* Or the classic, *You'd be so pretty if you smiled, Katya.*

My mother isn't much better. She started putting me on diets when I was eleven to "lose the baby fat." By the time I was in my teens, dear ol' Mom made a habit of making me stand in front of the mirror while she pointed out my "problem areas" and pinched the extra skin on my arms and waist.

I've known from an early age that I'm only worth what my father can get out of me. My role was to be the perfect doll, like my mom. I always fell short of their expectations, however. Too short, too chubby, too opinionated. Too much, yet never enough.

But when Valentino gently lifted up my shirt, I could see something close to reverence in his gaze. I thought I was making it up, but then he whispered that I was beautiful.

I was so caught off-guard that I didn't have time to respond before he got to work cleaning up my bandages. God, what a mess. I have no idea what Valentino is going to think of me this morning after everything that happened.

There's only one way to find out.

Swinging my legs over the edge of the bed, I take a deep breath and stand. I find a pair of socks and pull them on, smiling when they go halfway up my calves. I briefly think about finding some pants or shorts from Valentino, but I don't want to disturb him. Plus, the shirt I'm wearing is practically a dress.

I gather up my long black hair and twist it to the side, letting the strands flow over my left shoulder. Taking one last cleansing breath, I turn the doorknob and peek into the hallway, relieved to see I'm alone.

Tiptoeing out of my room, I head to the stairs and descend, pausing on the bottom step when I see Valentino in the kitchen. My palms grow sweaty and my heart kicks into high gear as I make my way in that direction.

He doesn't see me at first, giving me time to study his silhouette. Instead of a suit, Valentino is wearing joggers and a black t-shirt that stretches across his chest and showcases his thick biceps. He's casual today, which hopefully means he's starting to get more comfortable around me. I don't know what my future holds, but something tells me Valentino is going to be a very important person to me. He already is.

The far too sexy man pulls out a few boxes of something from a grocery bag, lining them up on the counter. Upon further inspection, I realize the boxes are different kinds of hot chocolate. My heart melts, even more so when Valentino opens another grocery bag and produces a huge bag of marshmallows.

"Will these do, princess?" he asks, startling me.

"You got me hot chocolate?" I whisper, looking between him and the boxes on the counter.

"I was thinking I might have some too, but yes."

I grin at him, and he returns it. Well, he tries to, anyway. It's going to take more than that to get a real smile out of him.

"I also picked up some clothes. I didn't know what to get, so the lady at the store just sort of filled my cart. The bags are in the living room."

"Valentino, I… You didn't have to do that," I whisper.

He shrugs, then looks away, concentrating heavily on the groceries instead of me. Is he embarrassed? It's kind of adorable. I take pity on him and bring the conversation back to the most important topic.

"There's just one problem," I say, tapping my chin as I look over the half-dozen varieties of hot chocolate. Valentino's brow furrows, making him look even more adorable. Not that I'd ever tell him that. "I prefer my hot chocolate with whipped cream and sprinkles. Like a princess," I tease, crossing my arms over my chest.

Valentino gives me a playful look, then empties the rest of the grocery bag onto the counter. He has three kinds of whipped cream, three different kinds of sprinkles, as well as mini chocolate chips, and mini butterscotch chips.

"Will this satisfy your sugar craving?" he asks, knowing full well he went above and beyond.

I nod once. "It will suffice," I declare, bringing a spark to Valentino's eyes. "Now, let's get to making some master-pieces," I say, rubbing my hands together as I survey my options.

Dark chocolate, white chocolate raspberry, milk chocolate and mint, caramel swirl, peanut butter chocolate, and candy cane hot chocolate all stare back at me. I open the dark chocolate box and pluck out a packet. Looking over my shoulder, I see Valentino standing there, shifting his weight from foot to foot.

"Which one do you want?" I ask, waving my hand in front of the selection.

"Uh, what do you recommend?"

"I mean, I like the dark chocolate, but you might be different. What have you had before? I can direct you to something similar."

Valentino looks up at the ceiling and lets out a sigh. "Can't say I've ever had hot chocolate," he admits.

"What?" I gasp in horror. My mouth drops as I stare at him. "Never?"

33

He shakes his head and shrugs. "I don't have room for such frivolous things in my life."

Ouch. Are we still talking about the hot chocolate? Or perhaps we've moved on to discussing me and how I need to get out of his hair.

"Right," I say after a beat of silence, hoping I don't sound too disappointed. "That makes sense."

"But then again, I've never tried to make room. Maybe hot chocolate would do me some good."

I can't contain the smile that stretches across my face. "Well, it certainly couldn't hurt."

Valentino flashes me a rare and radiant smile. I'll treasure it forever.

"Okay, then. I'll get to work on our drinks," I inform him, clapping my hands and rubbing them together. I need a hot chocolate concoction that will soften Valentino's defenses. No pressure.

He points to where the mugs are, along with a saucepan. I hum to myself as I heat up the milk on the stove, stirring constantly so it doesn't burn. Turning off the burner, I set the milk to the side to cool down a bit.

Pondering the perfect combination, I decide to stick with dark chocolate for both of us. We can branch out into the fancier flavors later. *If there is a later.* I shove that thought way down deep, unable to unpack why the thought of leaving physically pains me.

I stir the milk into the first mug, making sure to get rid of all the clumps of chocolate powder. Next, I grab the canned whipped cream and execute the perfect swirl right on top, followed by a dusting of rainbow sprinkles and a few strategically placed mini chocolate chips. I finish the decadent drink with a marshmallow nestled on top of the whipped cream, like a star on top of a Christmas tree.

I look over my shoulder to where Valentino is sitting at

the kitchen table, his eyes fixed on me. I should find it unnerving, but I like his attention. I want him to look at me, to praise me, to tell me I'm beautiful again.

As I approach the table, Valentino's gaze drops from mine to the beverage in my hand. His eyes go wide as I set it down in front of him, making me giggle.

"Holy shit," he mumbles.

"Too much?" I ask self-consciously, rocking back and forth on my heels.

Dammit. I should have scaled back, gone with something simpler. Of course, it's too–

"No," he's quick to respond. He sounds almost angry, but I don't think it's directed at me. Honestly, he sounds defensive, as if I'm going to take his drink away from him. That makes me light up from the inside. Valentino is so freaking cute, and he has no idea. "It's a masterpiece."

I'm sure my ecstatic smile is giving away all of my feelings for this man, but at this moment, I don't care. I watch intently as Valentino takes a sip, waiting for his approval.

"Sweetest thing I've ever tasted," he says.

"Is that… bad?"

"No. I expect nothing less from you, princess."

My eyebrows shoot up to my forehead at his words. What does that mean?

Valentino takes another sip, his eyes never leaving mine. I grin when he sets the mug down, pointing out his whipped cream mustache and dollop on the tip of his nose.

"Do I have something on my face?" he asks, a smirk pulling at his lips.

I nod, taking a step closer. Valentino scoots his chair back from the table and holds out his hand. I take it and let him draw me toward him until I'm standing in front of him, between his legs.

My heart thuds against my ribcage, each beat echoing throughout my chest and down my spine.

"Can you get it for me?" he rasps, never breaking eye contact.

I'm helpless to do anything other than obey. Reaching out, I swipe the cream off his nose and lick it off my finger without thinking about it. Valentino's eyes flash with something dark and fierce, but it's gone before I can be sure it was there in the first place.

My breathing grows shallow as I lift my hand to his face, and my fingers shake as they hover over his lips. I drag my thumb across his top lip, gathering up the whipped cream. Valentino surprises me by looping his fingers around my wrist and pulling my hand toward him.

His wicked gaze never leaves mine as he licks the whipped cream off of the tip of my thumb, grunting in approval before wrapping his lips around my digit and sucking.

"Valentino," I murmur, my breath caught in my throat.

"Katya," he growls, making me weak in the knees. "Come here, princess." He pats his lap and helps me straddle him, smoothing his hands up and down my bare thighs.

I steady myself with my hands on his shoulders, giggling when he bounces me once.

"God, what you do to me…" He trails off, sliding one hand up my spine until his fingers tangle in my hair. Tugging slightly, he pulls my head back, exposing my neck. Valentino ghosts his lips up and down my column, pausing to nip at an extra sensitive spot below my ear.

I squeeze my thighs around him, needing something. Needing everything, but not sure how to ask for it.

Valentino loosens his grip on my hair, dropping his hands to my hips and rocking me against his solid erection. I should be scandalized, right? But all I want is more. More of whatever this man has to offer.

"Need a taste," he says, his voice deep and gravelly.

I find myself nodding before he's finished his sentence. Leaning down, I meet him halfway, our lips finding each other in soft kisses until he drags my bottom lip through his teeth and dives into my mouth.

I moan as his tongue slides against mine and tickles the roof of my mouth. Each stroke winds me up tighter and tighter, and I grind my soaking wet center against his thick dick, a shudder running through me at how huge and hard it is.

We break for air, and Valentino rests his forehead on mine.

"Wow," I breathe. "That was… that was…"

"A mistake," he finishes for me.

A bucket of ice is thrown over me at his words. I scramble off of his lap and wrap my arms around my middle, protecting myself from him. Valentino looks angry and hurt at the same time.

"Do you really think that?" I whisper, trying to push back my tears until I'm alone.

"It doesn't matter what I think," he grits out. "It was wrong of me to take advantage. Inappropriate on all levels. Please accept my apology."

Double ouch.

I don't say anything, not trusting my voice at the moment. Valentino stands from his seat and clears his throat, adjusting himself so his erection isn't quite so prominent.

He clearly enjoyed himself, so what went wrong?

"Help yourself to anything in the kitchen," he says, the cold, aloof tone back in his voice. "I'm going to the gym downstairs and then off on an assignment. I probably won't see you the rest of the day."

I nod, blinking back tears.

"Listen, Katya…"

I hold my hand up, cutting him off. Valentino sighs, running a hand through his hair, then turns on his heel and stomps down the hallway, presumably toward the basement.

I'm left staring after Valentino, my fingers fluttering over my lips where I can still feel his kiss. I don't understand him at all. We made good progress with the hot chocolate, but then… I don't know. I honestly don't know what happened.

Maybe he's just as broken and scared as I am. Maybe it was intense for him, too. Like we shared more than just a kiss. He gave me a piece of his soul, and in return, Valentino kept a little piece of me.

Focusing on breakfast, I try to shake my head of those thoughts. Besides, I have my hot chocolate bar to devour. I'll just have to enjoy my time here for as long as it lasts.

CHAPTER FIVE

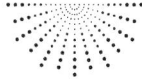

VALENTINO

I groan as hot water from the shower hits my skin, burning away the stress and confusion of the last few days. My muscles are sore, and not just from the grueling punishments I've put my body through at the gym several times a day. The pain is deeper than that. I ache everywhere, and I'm beginning to realize I won't feel better until I sort things out with Katya.

Goddamnit.

Pouring some body wash into the palm of my hand, I smooth it over my arms, chest, and torso, remembering the soft sweetness of her kiss. God, the way she gasped and moaned as I sipped from her lips, her luscious curves pressed against my hard muscles, her thighs spread out as she ground her hot little center over my...

Stop it, I shout at myself, though I know it won't help.

It's been three days since my world was flipped upside down with one little kiss. Three days since we've had a real conversation. Three days since I've touched, smelled or tasted her.

I successfully avoided Katya for the rest of that first day, though I worried about her having another nightmare. I set up camp outside her room until dawn, then caught a few hours of sleep before getting up for work.

Yesterday, Katya left the room any time I entered, refusing to make eye contact with me. Before leaving for the afternoon, I set out a fresh bandage and some vitamin E cream to help with scarring. I was half convinced she'd be gone when I came back. However, the bandage and lotion were gone from the table and the light was on in her room. There was evidence of freshly washed dishes drying in the rack as well. After a shower, I made my bed outside of her door again and settled in for another sleepless night.

I startled awake this morning around five when Katya got up to use the restroom. I barely made it back to my room before her door swung open. I don't know what I would have told her if she asked what the hell I was doing. When she was safely back in bed, I got dressed and slipped out of the house, needing to do something, anything other than deal with my thoughts and emotions.

Usually, throwing myself into work erases whatever bull-shit is going on in my life. But Katya is different. The more I try to ignore her, the more she pops into my head. Her smile, those fierce golden eyes, her soft skin, and silky hair… She's all I can fucking think about, and it's messing with me.

Yes, she's exquisite. With olive skin, midnight black hair, and eyes the color of honey, Katya is like a goddess of beauty and grace. But her looks are only a fraction of why I'm obsessed with her.

Katya has been surprising me since the moment I laid eyes on her. From jumping me and holding me at gunpoint to confessing her horrible situation while I patched her up without any anesthesia. There's no denying she's strong as fuck and determined to survive. She's incredibly resilient, tender, and sweet, even after everything she's been through.

I finish up my shower, grabbing a towel and drying off before throwing on jeans and a t-shirt. I've been home for over an hour but still haven't seen Katya. It's almost dinner time, so maybe I can lure her out with a meal. We need to talk, though I'm not sure if I'm going to tell her to find a new place to stay or sweep her off her feet with another earth-shattering kiss.

Only one way to find out.

When I'm halfway down the stairs, I hear her rustling around in the kitchen. Good. I won't have to hunt her down and force her to eat with me. The aroma of creamy alfredo and seasoned chicken wafts past me as I reach the bottom step, and my mouth is watering by the time I get to the kitchen.

Katya is stirring a pot on the stove, sashaying her hips as she hums to herself. She hasn't seen me yet, which gives me the opportunity to study her. The dark orange and pink light from the setting sun streams in through the kitchen window, reflecting off her hair like glitter as she sways.

Yeah, there's no way I'm kicking this woman out. I very much want to kiss her again, but I forgot about the third option; fall to one knee and beg her to be mine forever.

Reel it in, goddamnit.

"Katya," I say, my voice much rougher than I intended.

She gasps and spins around, her feet slipping on the tiled floor. I'm next to her in a second, wrapping an arm around her back and steadying her before she falls. Katya peers up at me, those brilliant eyes searing me all the way down to my soul.

A million thoughts fly through my head as I stare into her golden depths. *Stay, be mine, let me protect you, let me worship you, let me be the one person you can trust.*

Instead of confessing any of that, I help Katya regain her balance, then take a step back. As much as I want to wrap her up in my arms, I need to respect her space. I haven't exactly been easy to deal with, so I'm not sure how she feels about my presence.

"You made dinner?" I ask after clearing my throat.

Katya nods, nibbling her bottom lip while looking away from me. I hate it, but I only have myself to blame.

"Chicken alfredo," she answers, her voice soft, almost shy.

Where is the woman who asked me to serve her head on a platter to her father? Fuck. I hurt her more than I thought by pushing her away. I'm about to thank her, but she talks before I get a chance.

"Go sit down, I'll dish us up."

Nodding, I follow her orders. Katya piles homemade fettuccine noodles onto a plate, followed by a perfectly seared chicken breast, and topped with a ladle of alfredo sauce.

"This looks incredible," I tell her as she sets the food down in front of me.

She smiles briefly, but her eyes never meet mine.

"Thank you," I try again.

Katya nods once, then flits away to grab her plate.

Once we're both seated at the table, I dig into the meal this gorgeous woman prepared. After three or four bites, I notice Katya isn't eating. Pausing, I set my utensils down and look at her, tilting my head to the side. She's tapping her foot and wringing her hands under the table. The old me would have assumed she poisoned my meal and her nerves were getting the better of her.

Sitting here, looking at the anxious mafia princess fidgeting in her chair, I know the cause of her restlessness is all my fault. I've been a dick by avoiding her after kissing her. No wonder she doesn't know how to act around me.

"Listen, Katya–"

"I was thinking–"

We both speak at the same time, talking over each other.

"You go first," I offer, trying to give her a smile. It's rusty as hell and might do more damage than good.

Katya takes a deep breath and straightens her shoulders, lifting her chin like the proper princess she was taught to be. "I was thinking it's probably time for me to get out of your hair," she starts. My heart squeezes up painfully inside my chest, but I let her continue. "You've already done so much for me, and I know this dinner doesn't even begin to make up for it, but I guess think of it as an audition?"

I furrow my brow, not understanding her. "Audition?"

"I'm not explaining this well at all," she says under her breath to herself. I don't like seeing her frustrated and doubting herself. Katya clears her throat and starts again. "The last favor I'll ever ask of you is if you could point me in the direction of a Di Salvo business and give me a good reference?" Before I can even say anything, she raises her hands in defense. "Don't worry, no one will know it's me. I'll bleach my hair and wear contacts. Change my name. I'm guessing a lot of your bars and restaurants pay in cash under the table? That's exactly what I'm looking for."

"Katya–"

"Just until I make enough money to pay you back and save some for a bus ticket somewhere else. I can sleep in one of the warehouses, as you know. I won't mess with anything or disturb anyone. I'll be gone before you know it."

She blinks at me, tears welling up in her eyes, though she doesn't let them fall. This woman is ruining me.

"Katya–"

"Please," she whispers, her voice cracking.

I can't take it anymore.

Standing from my chair, I close the distance between us, my eyes never leaving Katya's as I kneel in front of her.

"You can't leave," I tell her softly, gathering her hands in mine. "Somehow, you've become essential to my being, and I can't let you go." Brushing my lips over her knuckles, I kiss each one before guiding her to place her hands on my shoulders.

"But I thought…" Katya trails off, confusion filling her eyes. "I thought it was a mistake. Everything. The kiss, bringing me into your home, caring for my wound. I thought you were done with me."

"Fuck, princess, I'm so sorry. I know I'm difficult and confusing, but honestly, I've never met anyone like you. Never had these intense feelings, never needed someone's safety and happiness more than my own. I didn't know what to do with you, with myself, really. You make me feel… raw and vulnerable, and that scares me."

"I scare you?" she murmurs, lifting one eyebrow in question.

"With you in my life, I have someone to lose. Someone to let down. Someone to hurt, even if by accident."

"You would also have someone who cares about you. Someone to share in the joys and the sorrows of life. Someone to encourage and support, someone who wants the best for you. If you only look at the darkness, you'll never see the light."

"What if I don't deserve your light?" I rasp, gliding my hands up her legs until my fingers wrap around her hips. "What if the darkness is all I've ever known?"

"Then trust me enough to show you what you've been missing."

Hope sparks in her ethereal eyes and soothes something in my chest. Slowly, I pull Katya to the edge of her seat, then wrap my arms around her and settle her down into my lap. She giggles, and the sound warms me like a ray of sunshine.

"I do trust you, Katya," I tell her, resting my forehead on hers. "But can you trust me? I've already let you down."

She cups the side of my cheek, her thumb lightly brushing over my stubble. "We're both broken," she whispers. "But I think together, we could heal."

"I would like that very much. Can you forgive me for being an asshole the last few days?"

A wicked grin curls up the corners of her lips, making me want to kiss it right off of her face.

"With enough hot chocolate, forgiveness is definitely in your future." Katya's eyes sparkle as she smiles at me, and I can't hold back any longer.

Leaning forward, I pull Katya's bottom lip through my teeth, then whisper, "Can I start making it up to you?"

"What did you have in mind?" Her voice is low and breathy, and she has no idea how sexy she is right now.

"First," I murmur, "I'd like to kiss you until we can't breathe."

"Mmhm," she says with a nod, rubbing her nose against mine. "I like that plan."

"Then," I continue, pressing a kiss to that sensitive spot below her ear, "I'd like to kiss you everywhere if you'll let me."

"Everywhere?" she practically whimpers.

"Yes, princess. You need it, don't you? Need me to make the ache go away?"

Katya nods, a strangled sound stuck in her throat as she grinds down on my lap.

"Fuck," I growl, cupping the back of her neck and drawing her down for a kiss.

I'm instantly lost in everything she's offering. Kayta opens up for me, her tongue chasing mine and letting me know she wants this as much as I do. She breaks the kiss to breathe, but I can't get enough of her sweet skin. I drag my nose and lips down her throat, then lick and nip my way back up to her ear, where I whisper, "Need to get you naked."

"Yes," she whispers, her chest heaving with labored breaths.

I somehow manage to tear myself away from Katya long enough to grab the hem of her shirt and help her take it off. As soon as the offending garment is out of the way, I run my fingers up and down her torso, over her breasts, her nipples, anywhere and everywhere I can reach.

Pausing to gently trace the bandage on her side, I peer up at her, silently asking if she's in pain. Katya smiles and shakes her head, leaning close to capture my lips. "I'm feeling much better," she murmurs once we break apart. "I know you'd never hurt me."

"Damn right," I grunt, licking a stripe up her throat.

Katya's desperate moans spur me on as I gently lay her on the floor, spreading out her gorgeous body so I can consume every inch. I bend down and suck on her tits, licking one pebbled peak and then the other, alternating until I feel her tremble beneath me. Fuck, her skin tastes like warm vanilla and feels impossibly smooth, like porcelain. I nibble on the underside of her generous breasts, more than a handful, just like her juicy ass, and continue exploring her body with my mouth.

I drag my lips over her torso, careful to avoid her bandage. The wound itself is well on its way to healing, but I still need to be careful with my precious girl.

"Valentino… oh God, it feels… it feels…"

"How does it feel, princess?" I growl into the soft flesh of her stomach.

"Like… like…" Katya gasps and bucks her hips, thrusting up as I kiss my way down to her dripping center. I pause when I get to the waistband of my boxers that she's wearing, gripping it with my teeth and letting it snap against her skin.

"Tell me how it feels," I demand.

"Like my skin is on fire," she whispers.

"What else?" I murmur as my fingers dip into the waistband and slowly pull the last piece of clothing down her legs, kissing her thighs and calves as I go.

"So much pressure. Valentino… please. It aches. I *ache* for you."

"Jesus," I breathe out through gritted teeth. "I can make the pain go away, Katya. Do you trust me?"

"I trust you, Valentino."

Her sweet words are surpassed only by the sweet scent of her pussy. I nuzzle into her dripping cunt, memorizing everything about how she feels, how she smells. Her soft curls tickle my nose, and the sensation makes my dick leak and throb in my pants. I dip my nose barely inside her wet slit. Goddamn, what this woman does to me, surrendering her sweet, innocent body to my sinful desires.

A strangled whimper falls from her lips, snapping the last thread of control I had. I lick up her sticky center, finding her swollen clit right away and lavishing it with attention. Her thighs snap against my head, but I pry them apart so I can taste more of her, all of her. It'll never be enough.

Katya twists and bucks her hips, trying to get me deeper. I lean back a bit and grin when she whines. Her protests die on her tongue when I drag a finger up and down her slit, circling her entrance.

I carefully push the tip of my middle finger inside her, groaning when her cunt squeezes and pulses around me. Jesus, fuck, she's *tight*. Holy hell.

"Valentino… oh! Ohmygod!"

I growl and lick her from top to bottom, flattening my tongue so I can taste and touch as much of her as possible. I feel her opening pulse underneath my tongue and more of her juices spill out.

She wants to be my dirty girl. I can feel it. Smell it. Taste it. Hear it in every ragged breath and broken cry. I swear I can see it written on her soul. She's mine. My innocent, filthy, perfect woman.

Katya tangles her fingers in my hair like she needs to steady herself. I slip my hands under her ass, gripping her cheeks and pulling her even closer to me while I eat out her little pussy in rough strokes and teasing bites.

"Something's happening… something is ha-happening to me."

"Let it happen," I growl, drawing her clit between my lips and sucking lightly. I let it go and bat it with the tip of my tongue and then lick. Hard.

"Ohmygod…" She presses her cunt into my mouth like she can't help it, rubbing her drenched folds all over my chin and tongue, whimpering like a sweet, confused angel. "It feels so good. And it aches, and… oh. *Oh!*"

She erupts in my mouth, her nails digging into my scalp as her trembles turn violent. Katya's throaty sobs of my name have me humping the goddamn floor to find some relief for my angry cock. I lap at her hungrily, not wanting a single drop of her pleasure to escape me. I made it. I own it. It's mine.

I shove one thick finger inside her, opening her up and giving her a taste of what's to come. Her pussy pulses around me, over and over, until I feel her relax on the floor completely. I remove my finger, chuckling as she gasps and shudders. I lick her essence off me and then gather her limp body into my arms, carrying her over to the couch.

I sit us down, then grab a blanket from the back of the couch, wrapping it around Katya's naked body. "Are you okay, princess?" I ask, kissing the top of her head.

"Oh my god, Valentino," she says in a raspy voice. "I've never… I mean, like… holy shit."

I chuckle at her response, loving her flushed cheeks and swollen lips. Her hair is mussed and her eyes shine with satisfaction and awe. I can't wait to see her like this again, only next time, she'll be spread out on my bed.

"So I can do that again?" I question, peering down at my worn-out, sexy-as-hell woman.

"Um, yes. Any time you want to… uh, do that, I would be appreciative," she slurs, tucking her head into the side of my neck.

I stroke her back, unable to help the smile stretching across my face. "Good," I murmur as her breathing grows steady and deep. "I'll need to start making up for lost time."

Katya doesn't answer, but I don't expect her to. Her cute little snores let me know she's resting after such an intense experience. I'll be right here when she wakes up.

CHAPTER SIX

KATYA

The timer goes off, and I hop off the couch, eager to frost the cupcakes I made now that they are officially cool enough. I can't wait to see Valentino's face when he sees the dessert I made for tonight. I figured if he hadn't had hot chocolate until a few days ago, he'd probably been missing out on the amazingness of cupcakes as well.

He left this morning for a "meeting," aka, an assignment from the Boss. While I don't love that he's in the same line of work as my father, I know deep down in my soul that Valentino is different. For one, he could barely stomach the story behind the cut on my side. I know he'd be livid on my behalf if I told him the other ways I've been abused in the past.

Valentino has also taken better care of me than anyone I've ever met. He had no reason to patch me up and provide shelter. In fact, I'm sure he broke protocol by taking me into his home. As far as I know, he hasn't told anyone else in the family that I'm here.

I've never had anyone be so protective of me, and I won't lie, I kind of love it.

I spread buttercream frosting over one double chocolate cupcake, then move on to the next. After three cupcakes have been frosted, I stop to add a few sprinkles on top. I don't want the frosting to harden too much, otherwise the sprinkles won't stick.

Just as I'm finishing up the last cupcake, I hear Valentino's car pull up in the driveway. My stomach flips and dissolves into a thousand butterflies swirling around in my gut. After everything that happened last night, our confessions, our kisses, and God, the way he touched me, licked me, commanded my body...

I'm hoping for a repeat. Actually, I'm hoping we go further tonight. I want to give Valentino all of me. I want him to be my first, and I pray that he'll be my only. Is that crazy?

Yes. Definitely yes. That doesn't seem to matter, though. I crave more of him, more of his heart, more of his body, more of his painful secrets he's carried by himself for so long.

The front door swings open, and my eyes immediately find Valentino's as he stalks through the living room toward me. I grin at him, unable to contain the giddiness I feel whenever he's in the room.

Valentino steps up behind me and circles his arms around my waist, nuzzling into the back of my neck while I finish putting sprinkles on the last cupcake. I spin around in his arms, capturing his lips in a heated kiss. He groans, tightening his hold on me and pressing my body impossibly closer to his.

"Katya..." he breathes, sounding almost in pain. "Love everything you do to me."

I look up at him and smirk as a wicked idea passes through my mind. Valentino lifts an eyebrow in question, but before he can say anything, I start unbuttoning his shirt. He hums in approval, his voice deep and filled with desire as I trail my fingers up and down his chiseled abs and defined chest.

I slide his shirt down his powerful shoulders and dip my finger in the bowl of frosting sitting next to me on the counter. Valentino's eyes grow wide, but he doesn't say anything as I trail a line starting at his sternum and ending right above his belly button.

Flattening my tongue against his hard stomach, I lick up toward his chest, never breaking eye contact.

"Fuck," he grunts before winding his fingers in my hair and tipping my head back so he can devour me.

Valentino grips the hem of my t-shirt and I lift my arms so he can take it off, revealing my bare breasts. Deciding to have some fun of his own, Valentino dips his fingers in frosting and circles one nipple and then the other. I shiver at the cool cream and then moan when he sucks it off of me.

"Is this what you wanted, princess? You want to drive me insane?"

"I was hoping to seduce you," I breathe, my voice caught in my throat as he sucks on my other breast and bites my nipple.

Valentino stops in his tracks and looks at me. "You've been seducing me since the very first moment I held you in my arms."

"Well, then, how about I finish the job tonight?"

Before he can say anything else, I reach for his pants and get his belt undone.

"Are you sure, Katya?" he asks, his voice tight with restraint.

I loop my fingers in the waistband of his pants and tug him closer to me while looking up at him. "I'm sure, Valentino. I want everything with you, and I want it starting tonight."

His eyes somehow manage to go soft yet sharp with arousal at the same time.

"Thank fuck," he growls. "I can't stay away from you anymore, princess."

"Then don't."

I hardly get the words out of my mouth before Valentino slides my pants down my legs.

"Damn, Katya. You weren't wearing panties or a bra all day today?" he asks while kneeling in front of me and massaging up my legs.

I shrug and smile down at him.

"Dirty girl," he grunts, kissing a trail from my belly button to the top of my pussy.

In one swift move, Valentino stands up with me in his arms and deposits me on the counter. He stands between my legs and kisses me urgently. When we break apart, I see a playful gleam in his eyes.

"You don't know what kind of game you've started," he says, his voice low and gravelly and sexy as fuck.

"Show me then," I reply.

Valentino gathers up some frosting on his fingers and trails a lazy path between my breasts, down to circle my belly button. He lifts his fingers to my mouth and I suck the remnants of the sugary frosting off of his digits, swirling my tongue and nipping the pads of his fingers. I love watching his pupils dilate with every swipe of my tongue.

He withdraws his fingers from my mouth and leans in to pull my bottom lip between his teeth. He peppers hungry nips and bites down my neck and my collarbone and then begins cleaning up the trail of frosting with his tongue. I lean back with my hands behind me on the counter to give him better access. I swear I can feel every swipe of his tongue on my clit.

When he's done, Valentino stands and guides me so I'm

lying down on the counter all the way. He sets my heels on the edge, opening my legs wide for him to see all of me.

"Fucking beautiful," he whispers more to himself than to me. His hands are all over me then, cupping my breasts, tickling down my curves, squeezing my thighs.

Valentino kneels so his face is right in front of my pussy. I close my eyes when I feel his warm breath across my wet opening and gasp when cool frosting coats my folds. Before I can even process the different sensations, Valentino eats up the frosting, using every part of his mouth on my soft, tender skin.

He growls into my cunt and nips at my clit, making my inner muscles contract and my legs snap around his head. I feel Valentino's tongue circle around my tight little hole and slowly push inside. His wicked tongue darts in and out of me and then circles my clit, again and again, working me up into a frenzy.

I hold my breath as the muscles in my back all tense up. I buck my hips and moan every time Valentino's tongue hits me just right, sending jolts of electricity through my body. Slowly, one finger slides into my cunt, and I squeeze around it tightly, making Valentino groan.

"It's going to feel fucking incredible to be inside you, princess."

He keeps pumping his finger in and out of me while sucking on my clit. Then there are two fingers stretching my tight channel, and with a sudden flick of his wrist, Valentino hits some spot inside of my cunt that has my orgasm slamming into me, my entire body curling in and then exploding with uncontrollable waves of pleasure, so intense I can't breathe.

Valentino doesn't stop, he doesn't let up for one second, he just licks me right through it, pushing my orgasm beyond anything I've experienced so far. His ruthless tongue drags across my tender flesh, lapping at my release. He growls and sucks on my pussy, making wet, sloppy noises. I can't get enough. Neither can he.

My back bows off the counter as Valentino grunts into my still-convulsing pussy and guides my legs over his shoulders. His hands slip underneath my ass and bring me impossibly closer to his mouth so he can lick me clean. My bones are liquid by the time he's done.

I'm vaguely aware of being lifted in Valentino's arms and carried into his room. When he sets me down, Valentino kisses my forehead, nose, and lips so sweetly. He cups my cheeks and rests his forehead on mine.

"Are you sure about this, Katya?"

I nod and place my hands on the outsides of his, looking into those intense, brown eyes that have so quickly become my home. "I trust you, Valentino. I want you. I can't wait any longer.

"I know, kitten," he says, kissing me deeply, brutally, and yet reverently. "I'm gonna make you feel so good, I promise," he whispers into the side of my neck before kissing me there.

Valentino skims his hands down my body and walks us toward the bed, where he gently pushes me down so I'm spread out before him.

Seeing how his body reacts to mine, how his gaze darkens and his cock hardens even more in the confines of his pants, makes me feel sexy and confident. I spread my legs wide and offer myself to him.

"Jesus," he grunts, ridding himself of the rest of his clothing. "So goddamn gorgeous. My beautiful, sexy girl giving me her delicious body…"

Valentino stands in front of me completely naked, and God, how I've missed looking at all of him. Feeling all of him. I sit up and reach out for his thick dick, but he catches my wrist and pulls it away.

"I'm afraid you've got me right on the edge. I swear if you breathe on me, I'm going to come, and I want this to last longer than that."

"Oh…" I blush, not sure what to say to that. "So… now what?" I wince at my ignorance.

Valentino cups my face and traces his thumb over my jaw. "Now you let me enjoy you. Let me have control, kitten. Let me make your first time incredible."

I nod and lean back on the bed, opening myself up again for him. Valentino takes another moment to look me up and down. I feel the heat of his gaze over my skin, my nipples, my lips, and then he locks his eyes on mine.

Never breaking eye contact, Valentino crawls on top of me and settles between my legs, rubbing his cock up and down my slit while resting his weight on his forearm beside my head.

"Ready?" he asks.

I nod and squeeze my eyes shut, preparing for the pain of losing my virginity.

"Hey, look at me, Katya," Valentino says so softly.

I open my eyes and see Valentino looking at me with such longing, such desire, but beyond that, I see the kindness and patience of the man I'm falling in love with. "I'm ready," I whisper.

He kisses me sweetly and lines himself up with my entrance. I feel the head of his cock stretching me wide open, and he's hardly inside of me yet. I tense and hold my breath.

Valentino stops and nuzzles the side of my neck. "Breathe, princess," he whispers in my ear. "I promise I'll take good care of you."

I take a deep breath and turn my head to kiss him while he surges forward, stretching me with his massive cock. I cry out and cling to him as he splits my body open.

"I'm sorry, love. You're doing so good. Are you okay?" His

tone is equal parts concern on my behalf and pained that he can't move. I'm struck again at the self-control this man has over his body so I can be comfortable.

"I'm okay, Valentino. I'm so… full. It doesn't hurt much anymore."

"Yeah?" he croaks, resting his forehead on mine.

I wiggle my hips, trying to get used to the feeling of him inside me. I like it. Not only how he makes my skin light on fire and my pussy throb in ways I couldn't even imagine a few minutes ago, but I like knowing we're as connected, as close as two people can possibly be. I'm already losing track of where I end and he begins.

"Move, Valentino. I need you to move."

"Fuck," he groans. "I don't want to hurt you, Katya."

I buck my hips and wrap my legs around him, taking him impossibly deeper. We both cry out with the rush of sensations, and a wave of wetness flows out of me.

"Please," I beg, wiggling my hips again.

He crushes my lips with his and pulls out of me, only to push back inside, hitting me deep. Valentino growls and fists my hair, tugging my neck up so he can kiss and bite me there. "You feel so damn good. This pussy was made for me," he grunts while picking up the pace.

I moan when his mouth moves over my breast, his tongue flicking at one pebbled nipple and then the other. My fingers weave in his hair to hold him to my chest while I arch my back, wanting to feel more of him, all of him.

Valentino slides one hand to the curve of my ass and then squeezes roughly, lifting my lower half to meet him thrust for thrust. Each time he hits home, my muscles tense, and I let out a little whimper. The pleasure feels unreal. My pussy walls flutter, my muscles shake, and my eyes burn with the effort of keeping all of these sensations inside me.

"That's it, Katya, come on my big fucking cock," Valentino demands.

My orgasm rises to the surface. It starts deep inside me, a pinpoint of bright light trickling throughout my body. Each ragged breath and rough stroke adds to that bright light until my whole being is engulfed in pure energy. Valentino slams into me, shocking my body into an intense orgasm. It feels like my chest is being ripped open as I scream and convulse in his arms.

When I come back down, Valentino kisses my forehead so gently, then nuzzles my neck.

"Can your gorgeous body take any more, princess?" he asks before pulling my earlobe through his teeth.

"Fuck…" I exhale. "Fuck, yes."

Valentino growls and pulls out of me, flipping me on my stomach and pulling my hips back. He squeezes and massages my ass cheeks before pulling them apart and stroking his cock up and down my slit, from my clit all the way to my puckered asshole. I shudder at the thought of him taking me there.

I should be scandalized, right? But instead, I'm absolutely *dripping* at the thought. As if reading my mind, Valentino leans over me, his muscled chest covering my back, and kisses between my shoulder blades.

"Not today, love. But soon, I'm going to have every inch of you."

I whimper and nod, suddenly feeling empty without him filling me up in some way. "I need you, Valentino," I beg, not caring if that makes me wanton or weak or slutty. I'll be slutty for him any time.

"Need you too, kitten," he grunts, slapping my ass once and then thrusting all the way inside me.

"*Fuck,*" I yell, gasping for air and digging my fingers into the mattress. "Oh fuck, you're so deep, so deep…"

I trail off, unable to complete the thought as Valentino pistons in and out of me, hitting that special spot with each powerful stroke of his fat cock. I press my body back into him, increasing the friction and causing us both to moan.

Valentino slides one arm under my hips to keep me in place while he fucks me savagely. His other hand skims up my back, the softness of his fingertips tickling up my spine intensified by the hard pounding he's giving me.

Valentino twists his fingers in my hair, pulling my head to the side so he can lean down and kiss me. His abs flex and tense against my lower back as he stuffs me full of his dick and tongue at the same time.

I bite his lip and he snarls into my mouth, making me even wetter for him.

"I want to feel you come like this," he says in a gravelly whisper before kissing the spot between my neck and shoulder.

Before I can respond, Valentino pinches my clit and bites my shoulder, making my pussy snap almost painfully tight around him.

"God fucking damn, I love feeling you squeeze my cock," he rasps.

I think he's going to come too, but instead, he pulls out and flips me back over, entering me again in one swift motion.

"Valentino!" I scream, coming again, or maybe still. I claw at his back as my body jerks, every movement sparking a deep, insatiable need.

"Katya," he grunts, holding himself up on one hand beside my head. His other hand grips my hip and steadies my trembling body as he buries his massive dick inside me again and again, tearing me apart ruthlessly in the best way possible.

Each stroke winds me up, up, up, my pleasure mounting into an almost unbearable orgasm. Everything goes white as my climax ravishes me from the inside out. My back bows, pressing my tits up against Valentino's hard muscles, and then I curl up in his arms, burying my head in his chest right as he roars his own release.

His arms give out and Valentino collapses on top of me, his large, warm body blanketing mine and keeping me sheltered from the storm of emotions and sensations rushing through my body. He tries to roll away, but I cling to him, needing his skin on my skin just a little bit longer.

"I don't want to crush you, princess," he chuckles into the side of my neck before kissing me there.

Valentino rolls to the side but keeps me in his arms, pressing me close to his body. My eyes are closed and I'm still shaking from my multiple orgasms, but Valentino slowly calms me down with the gentle touch of his fingertips swirling over my skin.

When I open my eyes, I'm floored by the look of awe in his deep brown gaze.

"That was…Jesus, that was amazing."

I nod and grin at him, giggling when he kisses all over my face. He tucks my hair behind my ear and presses his lips to mine, just savoring our closeness.

We stay like that for a while, on our sides, facing one another. Valentino runs his hand up and down my curves, tracing my outline, drawing me into being, giving me shape and purpose and meaning.

Eventually, Valentino readjusts us so he can pull the covers over our naked bodies. I curl up against his side, feeling safer and more loved than I can ever remember.

CHAPTER SEVEN

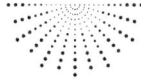

VALENTINO

"*What* the hell?" I mutter to myself as I pull the pan of what was supposed to be muffins out of the oven. Instead of having fluffy tops, these muffins are flat. How I managed to both burn the edges and undercook the center is a mystery to me.

So much for putting together a nice meal for Katya. She's made me hot chocolate, chicken alfredo, and cupcakes. It's only fair that I cook for her as well. Too bad I suck at anything culinary-related.

Growing up, my mom moved from one wealthy monster to another. We had chefs, so there was no need to learn how to cook. Once I escaped that prison at eighteen, I lived off whatever I could scrounge for until the Di Salvos picked me up and made me what I am today.

I'll just have to find a few easy recipes to start, then build my repertoire from there. I want to be able to provide my woman with everything, including her favorite meals.

I can't help the grin tugging at my lips. I sound like such a sap. I sound like someone I would have made fun of just a few short weeks ago. Actually, I remember telling our enforcer, Armando, that I couldn't understand his irrational attachment to Allegra. Seeing him, as well as Dante and Romeo find love was shocking and confusing to me. I didn't understand how one person could change your life so completely in the blink of an eye, or how priorities shift when you find someone worth keeping.

My situation is different from theirs, however. Katya is an enemy of the family, and a powerful one at that. She could be an important bargaining chip or give us intel on her father and his men. There are about a dozen things I should have done once I figured out who was squatting in the warehouse, but I couldn't bring myself to do any of them. I just… knew she was mine. Even back then, when I was fighting it with every cell in my body.

What the hell am I going to do? I've been wracking my mind for a solution, but can't seem to think of a way to keep Katya and my position within the family.

Usually, I'd talk to Armando about any problems I'm having, or Romeo himself if the occasion called for it. I trust both men with my life, and I wouldn't be in the inner circle if they didn't trust me with theirs.

I can't talk to anyone from the Di Salvos about this. Not until I have a plan.

Walking out of the kitchen, I peer up the stairs, listening for any sounds indicating Katya is awake. She was sleeping so soundly when I got up this morning, I couldn't bring myself to disturb her. She looked absolutely angelic with the golden morning light pouring over her soft skin and high-lighting her curves.

She must still be asleep, which makes me smirk. We wore each other out last night, and she deserves her rest.

Satisfied that I have a little while until she wakes up, I grab my phone from the counter and call one of two friends I have outside of the family. It rings a few times, and I pace around my kitchen, trying to decide if I should hang up and not bother with it.

"Val?" comes a raspy voice slurred with sleep.

Hawk is the only person who can call me that and get away with it. We've known each other for most of our lives, and everyone called me Val growing up. When I left that life, I left Val behind. I've been Valentino ever since.

"You there?" he asks.

"Yeah," I answer, clearing my throat.

"Everything okay? What fuckin' time is it?"

"Uh…"

"Seven-thirty in the morning? Not cool," he groans dramatically. I can just picture him running a hand through his messy hair as he flops back down on his bed. He never was a morning person, even before he joined the Savage Saints MC.

"Not all of us party at the clubhouse until three in the morning," I counter.

"I haven't lived that life for years and you know it," he grouses. "Besides, are you really trying to argue the moral high ground between the mafia and an outlaw MC?"

"No, I'm just giving you shit because you're easy to rile up."

"Remind me why I'm your friend?" he mutters, though I know he's mostly over it.

He doesn't stay upset for long. Despite being a high-ranking member of Savage Saints, Hawk is basically a golden retriever. Maybe that should have been his road name instead of Hawk.

"Because it's good to have friends in low places," I tease.

Hawk grunts then lets out a chuckle. "So what's up, Val? Why the early morning wake-up call?"

I sigh as I continue to circle around the kitchen restlessly.

"I have a… situation," I start. "A sensitive situation that I couldn't trust anyone else with."

My friend hums over the line, and I can tell he's focused on the conversation now. We give each other shit, but at the end of the day, we'll always have each other's back.

"There's a woman. She's… well, she's important to me. I think she's it. Like, the one or whatever sappy bullshit you want to call it."

I'm expecting Hawk to come in with a jab about falling in love, but he's surprisingly quiet. Strange.

"But she's also the daughter of our rivals. She ran away from her family, straight across enemy lines and into our territory. I should have called the Boss when I found her, but I just…"

"Couldn't let him decide her fate," Hawk finishes for me.

"Exactly. And now I don't know what the hell to do."

We're silent for a few moments, then Hawk clears his throat and whispers, "Believe it or not, I'm in a similar situation. Not the same, but there's this new waitress at the clubhouse, and she… Well, it's not about that right now," he cuts himself off. "Have you thought about telling the Boss? Maybe he'll understand."

"Are you going to tell the President of Savage Saints about your mysterious waitress situation?" I counter.

"I said it wasn't the same. Also, you're the one who called me, remember?"

I grunt in response, making Hawk laugh. "I need to figure out how to prove my loyalty and hat Katya is on our side. Tensions are high right now. We're on the razor's edge of an all-out war, and I've been harboring the enemy for over a week."

"Damn," he says, followed by a low whistle. "Have you talked to your woman about this? Katya, right?"

"Yeah. Well, no. I mean, she knows the situation, so what is there to talk about?"

"*This*," he answers emphatically. "This conversation. You know I appreciate your calls and your friendship, but these are the decisions you make as a couple. Share your fears and then figure out how to support each other and all that shit."

I chuckle. "I was calling for advice on handling my boss, and here you are, doling out relationship tips."

"Yeah, yeah, don't mention it," he jokes. "Just remember to send me an invite to the wedding. It's been a long time since I've visited NYC."

"Same to you and your waitress. Can't say I'll be thrilled to get gravel dust on my three-piece suit, but these are the kinds of sacrifices I make for our friendship."

Hawk laughs, and we say our goodbyes. No sooner do I set down the phone than the sweet, sleepy voice of my princess filters into the kitchen.

"Did you make breakfast?" she asks.

I spin around, my eyes roaming over Katya's body. She's in one of my shirts again, her hair a bit messy in the sexiest way, and a smile on her face that I'll never forget.

How is she this perfect combination of sweet, sassy, and drop-dead gorgeous? I don't know, but I'd like to spend the rest of my life figuring it out.

"I attempted to," I reply, tearing my gaze away from her to frown at the pan of ruined muffins. "But it turns out I'm not a baker."

Katya giggles, the sound lighter than air as it floats around the kitchen. She steps closer, rocking back and forth on her heels as those golden eyes meet mine. "I can teach you some things if you'd like," she says, leaning forward until her lips are barely an inch from mine.

"Only if I get to teach you a few things, too," I murmur, my tone deep and desperate.

"Like what?" Katya whispers, her breath tickling my lips.

I growl and take her hips in my hands, pulling her into my body and rubbing her soft belly up against my rock-hard cock. How is it possible to miss her already? I was inside of her less than eight hours ago, and yet everything in me is pulsing, panting, crying out for more.

"Like how much pleasure your curvy little body can handle and how many ways I can get you to come for me."

Katya moans and tilts her head back so I can bite and suck her sensitive skin. Her fingernails claw down my bare chest, and then she tugs at the waistband of my sweatpants to undress me, giving me permission to do the same to her.

I should slow down and make sure she's not too sore after last night, but one look in her hungry eyes lets me know she doesn't need my words, she needs my actions.

It's now my job to give Katya everything she's ever wanted, starting with my swollen fucking cock.

Gripping her hips, I spin her around so she's facing the kitchen counter. I nibble on her pulse point and lick away the sting before grazing my lips on the shell of her ear.

"Hands on the counter, princess. Bend over and show me that ass."

Katya moans and bends over, giving me permission to fulfill my deepest desire. I smooth my hands over the soft, porcelain skin of her ass, admiring everything about this goddess. She turns, looking at me over her shoulder. The image almost does me in, almost makes me burst on the spot.

"Are you going to fuck me, or just look at me?" Katya lifts a sassy eyebrow in challenge.

I remove my hands and then bring one down to smack her bare ass cheek, loving the way it jiggles and turns pink.

"Ah!" she yelps in surprise.

"That's for sassing me, Katya."

She glares at me, and I spank her again, watching her eyes

close and listening to the way her breath hitches when I make contact.

"You like that?" I grunt, massaging the sting away.

"Mmmm," she purrs as I continue to rub her heated flesh.

Sliding a hand down her front, I dip my fingers into her soaking wet pussy, chuckling darkly as I slowly circle her clit.

"Please, Valentino," she begs. "I need it. I need you."

Fuck, I need her too.

I whip out my dick and tease her entrance, running the head up and down her seam, collecting her sweet honey. Grabbing her hips, I position myself at her entrance and slam into her. Hard.

It takes everything in me not to come the instant I'm inside her. I pull out and thrust back inside one inch at a time, feeling the way her tight entrance stretches and pulses around me as I surge forward.

Katya bucks her hips, fucking me right back as we set a relentless pace. My hands slide from her hips and grab her ass cheeks, pulling them apart so I can see her pussy swallow my cock with each thrust. I keep rolling my hips, pounding into her as I feel my orgasm ready to rip through me.

I reach around and rub her clit, needing her to come first. Katya lets out a loud moan, her entire body tensing and spasming beneath me. I hook my other arm under her hips, holding her in place while I rut into her, barreling toward oblivion.

"Come on, baby," I grunt into the shell of her ear. "Come for me. Come so fucking hard."

I sink my teeth into her shoulder and she snaps, convulsing in my arms and shaking all over. Her pussy chokes my cock so fucking tight. It's amazing. I want to stay right here, on the edge of bliss, watching her convulse around my huge dick.

But I can't hang on another second. I thrust into her one

last time and explode, painting her pussy with my sticky cum. I continue to pump into her as she pulses around me again, my release triggering another earthquake inside her.

Katya's arms shake as she holds herself up on the counter, and I cover her with my body, placing my arms on either side of hers. We're both sweaty and panting as we slowly float back down to earth.

I tuck myself back inside my sweatpants, then turn Katya around, sliding her shirt over her arms and head. She's barely standing on her own, and I chuckle as I gather her limp body up and carry her over to the couch.

As soon as I sit down, my princess curls up against my chest, resting her head on my shoulder. I smooth her hair away from her face, then trail my fingertips across her neck, over her shoulder, and down her arm before reversing my path.

Katya relaxes completely, the tension draining from her muscles the longer I hold her.

"Valentino?" she whispers.

"Yes, princess?" I ask softly, continuing to stroke her side and neck.

"Earlier, when you were first bandaging me up, you said you learned at a young age how to take care of wounds." My breath catches in my throat, but I manage to swallow it down and give her a nod. "Can you tell me what happened? I just… I just want to know you. Everything about you."

She blinks up at me, and I'm struck by her purity, her goodness and light even though life hasn't been kind to her. Katya is dealing with so much, and yet she's making space to take on my burdens as well. She's truly incredible. I don't deserve her, but Katya is mine now, and I'm keeping her.

Leaning forward slightly, I press a kiss to her forehead and nose, savoring the connection before spilling my heart out to the only woman who has ever mattered to me.

"My dad took off when I was a kid, leaving me with my shallow, social-climbing mother. Her second husband was a bank president with a penchant for whiskey. He wasn't so bad, but his money ran out too quickly for my mother's growing appetite for the finer things."

I roll my eyes and scoff, remembering the day my mom and I moved out of the three-story mansion we'd been staying at for the last year. Katya runs her fingers over my collarbone, tracing my tattoos as she listens.

"She moved on to a hedge fund manager and strung him along for over a year, getting him to buy us a condo in Midtown while she cheated on him the entire time. After she milked him for all she could, dear ol' Mom was breaking her way into the upper echelons of society. That's when she doubled down on finding men who were richer than God and meaner than the devil."

"I'm so sorry," Katya whispers, her amber eyes peering into my very soul and comforting me on a deeper level than I knew possible.

I kiss her forehead before continuing. "I couldn't protect her when I was a kid. I tried, only to get tossed into a wall or beaten with a belt buckle. That's when I learned all I could about first aid. If I couldn't prevent the beatings, at least I could clean up the aftermath."

Katya gasps, her eyes filling with tears.

"Don't cry for me, sweet girl," I murmur. "I got my vengeance. After a decade of putting up with one abusive asshole after another, I beat the living shit out of the man we were living with at the time. I begged my mother to come with me, to leave the monstrous men of her past behind. But she refused. She told me… ah, fuck, princess. I don't mean to weigh you down with all of this."

"I want to know," she insists. "I asked, didn't I? Plus,

you've listened to all of my life problems for the last week. It's only fair to share some of yours."

I nod, then cup the back of her neck, pulling her in for a soft kiss. I hope she can feel how much this means to me, how our souls are now tied together forever.

Looking away from Katya, I take a deep breath and let out the last of my pitiful tale. "My mother told me everything in life comes at a price. Her highest goal was wealth, and she willingly sacrificed her health and safety to attain it."

"But *you* didn't have a choice!" Katya says with a surprising amount of anger. "Your mom had no right to sacrifice *your* safety for the sake of living the high life. How dare she?!"

I didn't think it was possible to smile after talking about such personal, painful things, but seeing my woman all worked up and ready to defend me has a grin pulling at my lips.

"I told her the exact same thing before walking away for good," I murmur. "My mother knows she can call me if and when she's ready to start a new life, but I'm not holding my breath."

Katya rests her forehead on mine, her hand coming up to cover my heart. "Thank you for sharing that with me," she whispers. "So, how did you end up with the Di Salvos?"

Gathering her hand up in mine, I kiss her knuckles before setting it back down on my chest. "I had nothing and no one, but I knew there was one place an Italian down on his luck could find work. Down by the docks."

She nods, knowing what I mean. That's where hopefuls line up to be recruited. If they complete an assignment quickly and efficiently, they get another one. And another. Until they're either proven too weak to stomach the life or promoted out of the rank of recruit.

"I got my first assignment when I was eighteen, promoted

to soldier at twenty, and then made Capo at twenty-five when I was given my own territory to manage. Last year, I joined the top-ranking officials in the inner circle. I…" I trail off, not sure why I said all of that.

"You've worked so hard to get to where you are today," Katya says softly. "And now…" she shrugs and looks away from me, but I'm not having any of that.

Cupping her chin, I gently turn her so she's facing me again. "And now?"

"I'm ruining everything," she chokes out, tears streaming down her cheeks. "I showed up and complicated your life, and now I'm ruining everything you've built. I'm sor–"

"Don't you dare apologize," I warn her, tucking a few strands of hair behind her ear. "You're not ruining anything. You have no idea how much you mean to me."

"But I'm the enemy. How can this possibly end well?"

"You're not the enemy," I growl, not liking those words coming out of her mouth. "I know things seem… unclear right now, but we'll figure it out."

"You'll lose everything, Valentino."

"The only way I could lose everything is if you walk away from me," I murmur, locking my eyes on hers. "I love you, Katya. I love everything about you. I love how strong you are in the face of danger and how selfless you are, even when you're hurting. I love your smile and laughter, the taste of your kisses, and your sinful curves. Princess, I'm afraid I can't let you go. I won't."

"You… love me?" she asks, disbelief evident in her gaze. Katya sniffles, her brow furrowing as she studies me.

"More than you could ever know," I promise.

A brilliant smile lights up her face, even with tears still falling down her cheeks. She's sunshine and rain and every-thing my dormant heart needs to grow.

"I love you, too, for the record."

"Say it again," I grunt, clenching my jaw as I stare at her lips.

"I love you, Valentino. I can't believe it's true, but I just… you make me feel so safe and wanted for the first time in my life. I don't think anyone has ever called me beautiful before. I didn't believe you when you said it to me the first time."

"Katya," I rasp, hating that she's had so little love and acknowledgment in her life. I vow to compliment her at least ten times a day until she starts to see herself through my eyes. And then I'll just keep on reminding her of her worth every single day for the rest of our lives.

"But you've shown me with your actions, your words, your entire being how much you care for me. I want to be the same for you. I love you."

I take her lips in a gentle kiss that turns heated quickly. Our tongues tangle, our breaths mingling as we pour out everything we can't say. Right as I start to slide my hands up Katya's shirt, my phone rings. I groan, breaking our kiss, while Katya continues to nibble my neck and chest.

"God, you feel so good," I breathe, hissing when she claws down my chest.

My phone rings again, and I know I need to answer it. Dante has been checking in on me a lot more the last few days. I'm trying not to be paranoid, but I'm starting to think he suspects me of betraying the family.

A third ring finally breaks my lustful haze enough to lean back and help Katya off my lap.

"Sorry, I should really take this."

She nods in understanding, but I know she's anxious.

By the time I reach my phone, the call went to voicemail. Shit.

A second later, a text pops up on the screen from Dante.

Come to the compound ASAP.

Double shit.

"Everything okay?" Katya asks from her position on the couch.

"Yeah," I choke out. "Fine." She frowns at me. "I need to go into work. Important meeting just came up."

"Do you think…?"

She doesn't have to finish the sentence for me to know what she's asking. Do I think it's about us?

"No," I tell her, though I'm not so sure. I've taken off at odd hours the last week, and I know Dante keeps meticulous notes on all of that shit.

"For a made man, you kind of suck at lying," she sasses.

I grin at her and shake my head. "Whatever the meeting is about, I can handle it. Oh, I'll bring home breakfast for us since I screwed up the muffins."

Katya nods, though I can see the tension in her eyes. She's worried about me, and I can't say that's ever happened before.

I clean up and change into a suit in record time. The sooner I leave, the sooner I can get back to my woman. I know she'll be anxious the whole time I'm gone.

"Everything will be okay," I tell her before kissing the top of her head. She's still on the couch, wrapped up in a blanket. "Watch some TV and I'll be back before you know it."

"You better be," she says, trying to sound tough.

I give her one last kiss, keeping it brief, otherwise I'll strip both of us naked and take her again. There will be time for that when I get back. Hopefully.

CHAPTER EIGHT

KATYA

*A*s soon as I hear Valentino's car pulling out of the driveway, I hop off the couch and sprint to the guest room I've been staying in. Rummaging around in the pile of clothes I came here in a week ago, I search for the nondescript notebook I stole from my father's office before sneaking out last week.

It was a last-minute decision, and I knew it was risky, but now I'm glad I made the effort. I'm positive he has no idea it was me, even if the timing matches up.

When my father wasn't yelling at me or teaching me a lesson with the back of his hand, he ignored me. I could be in the same room, sitting at the same table, and he would have no idea I was there. He didn't see me unless there was a problem. I spent most of my life resenting him for his heartlessness, but in this case, it worked out to my advantage.

I overheard him multiple times arguing with his second-in-command about keeping records. My father was insistent that there should be only one copy of the most important documents, and it would be handwritten. Otherwise, according to him, anyone could get their hands on it. No matter how many times they tried to tell him things were more secure than ever online, he never caved.

Pride comes before the fall, as they say. And what a fall it will be.

"Yes," I whisper to myself when my fingers graze across the cover of the small notebook. I tucked it in my bra for safe keeping, and luckily, was able to keep it hidden.

My stomach twists itself into knots at the thought of keeping a secret from Valentino. I hope when all is said and done, he'll understand why it had to be this way.

I quickly throw on a pair of leggings, a tank top, and a zip-up hoodie, slipping the notebook into the pocket of the oversized sweatshirt. I make my way downstairs, pausing in the kitchen where I saw a change jar tucked away in the corner of the counter. Dumping half of it out, I pick through the quarters until I have about twenty-five dollars. I'm hoping that will be enough to get me to the Di Salvo compound using public transportation.

A bus ride, a subway venture, and another bus ride later, I'm about a mile away from the compound. At least, I hope. My father has a section in his notebook for addresses and phone numbers of enemies, including the compounds of all the rival families in the city.

I'm not quite sure what my plan is, only that I have to do something. Valentino said he could handle the meeting on his own. He also said it wasn't about us, but I saw the doubt in his gaze as he told me both of those lies.

He's trying so hard to protect me, but who is going to protect him? I wish he would have talked to me about a plan for handling this instead of leaving me to take care of it himself.

I take calming breaths as I continue walking through the remote neighborhood containing the Di Salvo compound. The magnificent mansions grow farther and farther apart until I come across a large fortress surrounded by gates, cameras, and guards.

Bingo.

Shoring up the last of my courage, I straighten my spine, press my shoulders back, and lift my chin as I stride toward the front gate. The two guards out front take notice right away. One of them says something into the walkie-talkie attached to his shoulder while the other widens his stance and rests his hand on the gun tucked into his jacket.

I continue walking forward, my head held high, projecting a confidence I don't feel. I can see the moment they recognize me. Both men turn to each other, a look of disbelief and confusion shared between them.

I know they won't shoot me now they know I'm royalty. I'm too high up the food chain for them to pull the trigger without an order. Raising my hands in surrender, I continue moving forward until one of the men grabs my wrists, gathering them up in his large hand and holding them behind my back.

"What's a little Colombo princess doing so far away from her father's castle?" he sneers.

"That's between Romeo and me," I reply in a crisp tone.

The other man grunts, and the two exchange a glance and a nod. He stays put while the first guard shoves me forward, nearly making me fall on my face.

"Right this way, your highness," he says in a mocking tone.

I'm dragged through the house until I stand in front of a set of double doors made of solid oak and accented with gold. The guard pounds his fist on the door twice, then clears his throat.

"Boss? I've got a visitor here for you. You're going to want to talk to her."

"I don't have time," comes the harsh voice of who I assume is Romeo Di Salvo.

The guard is about to knock again, and I use the momentary distraction to pry my wrists from his death grip and lunge forward, grabbing the door handles and pulling them with all my might. The doors fly open, catching me off balance as I stumble inside the room.

My eyes are immediately drawn to Valentino, who jumps to his feet at the sight of me. Two other men I don't recognize are seated on the opposite side of the room. Before Valentino can say anything, I fix my gaze on Romeo, staring into his dark brown eyes and pleading with him to hear me out. "I'm Katya Colombo, and I ran away from my family over a week ago. I don't want anything to do with them anymore."

Romeo's eyebrows twitch upward slightly before he gains control of his features. Aside from that, his face is one of practiced indifference. "And why should we believe you?"

"Because—"

"I can vouch for her," Valentino says, stepping up next to me. I glare at him, and he glares back.

"I'm doing this to save you," I hiss at him. "Stop ruining it!"

Valentino doesn't back away. Instead, he wraps an arm around my waist and tucks me into his side. "If we go down, we go down together, princess."

"Someone better tell me what the fuck is going on," Romeo commands, his voice hard as granite.

"It's not Valentino's fault. Please don't blame him," I start, focusing on the Boss. "I ran away last week, and he found me."

"Katya," Valentino warns, but I keep going. I have no choice now. I jumped off the edge of a canyon, and I'm praying to every god I can think of that I land on the other side.

"Don't tell me she was the squatter in the warehouse," Romeo grits out, cutting a fierce glance at Valentino.

"I can explain," Valentino hedges.

"I was hurt," I jump in. "Bleeding real bad."

"My men roughed you up?" Romeo asks, some of the bite gone from his tone.

I'll never get used to people being upset over me getting hurt. Even though I'm part of a rival family, these men have a moral code not to harm me unnecessarily.

"No, the damage had already been done," I answer, looking away from him. I feel weak and stupid, but I press on, knowing that my mission is life or death. "By a man my father promised me to. I knew running away was risky, but I'd rather die fighting for my freedom than live with that abusive piece of shit day in and day out."

Valentino squeezes me closer to his side, turning his head so he can press his lips to my temple. I'm shaking from head to toe, but my man is right here with me, giving me the strength to continue.

"And you've been staying with…?"

"Me," Valentino responds. "I should have told you sooner, I just didn't know what to do," he says, bowing his head in deference to the Don. "She's already been through so much," he adds.

Romeo grunts, nodding his head once. "Why did you come here today, Katya? Why risk your life and your current set-up with Valentino? What's the advantage?"

"I couldn't live with myself if Valentino was harmed because he saved me, and it was only going to be a matter of time before the truth came out. But I have something important I hope you'll take in exchange for sparing Valentino."

"What?" Valentino whispers in my ear. "What are you doing, baby?"

"Something I should have done when you first found me," I whisper back. "I didn't know who I could trust, but I know now I should have trusted you. It's the only way I could think of to help."

Romeo clears his throat, and we both turn back to him.

I pull the little notebook out of my sweatshirt pocket, holding it out for Romeo to see. "I stole this before I left. My idiot father doesn't trust computers or the internet, so he keeps his most important notes written in here," I inform him, shaking the notebook for emphasis. "It's how I found your compound. It also contains numbers and addresses for numerous friends and foes, as well as coordinates for all kinds of weapons and storehouses."

The Boss raises an eyebrow, then holds out his hand.

I hold the notebook out slightly above his open palm, then stare at him directly in the eye. "If I give you this, you promise not to punish Valentino for being nice to me, right?"

"I'm not being nice to you," Valentino grumbles. "I fucking love you."

This startles the other two men in the room, as well as Romeo. For a brief moment, the infamous mafia boss looks surprised, followed by a flash of a smile, but he schools his face over before I can be sure what I saw.

"Usually, I don't negotiate," Romeo answers. "Especially with a Colombo."

Valentino growls softly, and I nudge him with my hip to shut up.

"And Valentino and I will need to have a chat about hiding things from me," Romeo continues. "But if what you say is true, and if Valentino's confession of love is real, then yes, we have a deal."

"Take me instead," I ramble, my mind still playing catch-up with the conversation. "Don't hurt Valentino. He's a good man."

"Katya, he said–"

"I'll lure my father out for you," I offer, scrambling to think of some way I can be valuable to Romeo. "I can–"

"Katya." This time, it's Romeo who says my name.

My eyes snap to his, my heart rattling around in my ribcage the longer I look at him.

"I said we had a deal."

"Wh-what? Really?" I blink at Romeo, not sure if this is all some cruel joke.

"Is that so hard to believe?"

"Yes," I answer truthfully. This earns me a smirk from Romeo. "I don't think anyone has ever listened to me."

Valentino kisses my temple again and whispers, "We're different from your family."

"That's a shame," Romeo finally says. "From what I can tell, you're brave, bold, and strong enough to fight for the life you want. You're clearly loyal to Valentino, even willing to offer your life for his. Those are excellent qualities for any mafioso to have."

A rush of emotions sweeps through me, stealing the breath from my lungs. "Thank you," I murmur, bowing my head at his compliment.

I place the notebook in Romeo's hand, then look over my shoulder at Valentino.

He spins me around in his arms and gathers me against his chest, nuzzling into the top of my head. "You should have told me what you were going to do," he whispers.

"You wouldn't have let me go through with it," I counter.

"Of course not."

"Well, goddamn," Romeo says, followed by a low whistle. He flips through a few more pages of the notebook, then looks around the room. "Jackpot, men. We have the location of their latest weapons haul."

He rattles off the address, and one of the men starts making notes on his laptop. I peer over at the other man who has been sitting in the corner, not saying a word. He has a goofy grin on his face, shaking his head at Valentino.

"Told you love would hit you in the chest like a lead pipe," the man says.

Valentino chuckles. "You also said not to fight it. Took me a little bit on that last part, but now that we're here…" He trails off, his gaze wandering back to me. "I wouldn't have it any other way."

I beam up at him, still not quite believing it all worked out. As if sensing my thoughts, Valentino hugs me closer, wrapping his arms around my back and stroking up and down my spine.

"We good here, Boss?" Valentino asks.

"What?" he grunts, his nose still buried in the notebook. "Oh. Yes, you two may go. Dante and I will go over the rest of these notes and have a plan of attack soon."

"Thank you," I say as Valentino takes my hand and starts pulling me toward the door.

Romeo nods. "Your loyalty will be tested in the days to come. This is a good start," he says, holding out the notebook.

"I won't back down," I tell him, clenching my jaw. "I'll fight beside you until every last one of my father's men is taken out."

"The hell you will," Valentino grunts.

I roll my eyes at him, which makes the other three men in the room laugh.

Without another word, Valentino tugs me the rest of the way out into the hall, then scoops me up in his arms, bridal style. I giggle and kick out my legs as he races toward the front door and down the porch steps.

"Where are we going?" I ask as he sets me down in front of his car. Valentino helps me into the passenger seat, then buckles my seatbelt before kissing my forehead.

"Need to get you home. Need to feel you, princess. All of you. Jesus, you scared me."

I cup his cheeks, drawing his face closer to mine. "I didn't mean to scare you. I just knew I had to do something."

"And now it's my turn to do something," he says with a wicked grin.

Valentino closes my door and hurries around to the driver's side, hopping in and peeling out of the Di Salvo compound.

CHAPTER NINE

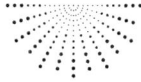

VALENTINO

*A*s soon as we get inside, I spin Katya around, pressing her against the closed door before crashing my lips down on hers. She grabs my shirt and pulls me closer as she sucks on my tongue, welcoming my kiss and fighting me for control.

"You shouldn't have put yourself at risk like that," I rasp before sucking on her neck.

"You would have done the same for me," Katya breathes, tipping her head back to give me more access to her creamy skin.

I glide my tongue over her flesh, nipping the sensitive spot below her ear before kissing away the sting. "It would have been a worthy sacrifice," I murmur, leaning back a bit to look her in the eyes. "But your life for mine? That doesn't make sense."

She furrows her brow in confusion, a heartbreaking look taking over her features. "Do you really think you're worth so little?"

"I… Well, I…" I look away from her, not sure how to answer.

Katya lays her palm gently against the side of my cheek, directing my gaze back to hers. "You're my whole world, Valentino. Whatever protective feelings you have for me, I also have them for you. Is that so hard to believe?"

"Yes," I answer truthfully, my voice hardly above a whisper. "But I believe you. I want to be the man you think I am. I want to be better for you, Katya."

"You're already so good to me," she says softly, her lips brushing against mine.

I welcome her kiss, letting her take the lead and falling under her spell once more. She writhes against my body, her nails digging into the back of my neck as she clings to me.

"Katya," I groan, resting my forehead against hers.

"Need you," she pleads, her voice breathy and laced with an undeniable urgency.

I growl into her lips, biting and nipping at her before licking into her mouth. My hands slide up the shirt she's wearing, pushing the fabric up as I feel every inch of her soft, porcelain skin. She moans and drags her hands down my chest, her fingers tugging at my belt and then working my button and zipper open. Katya grips my hard as fuck dick, pulling me out and pumping me roughly.

"Fuck," I groan, loving the fact that she's this needy, this turned-on, and this desperate for me. The thought makes me grunt possessively as I peel off her leggings, my hands finding the little lacy scrap of fabric covering her pussy. I rip it off her body and swallow her gasp as my fingers slide through her folds.

Goddamn, she's *soaked* for me, her cream dripping over my fingers and pooling in my hand. I circle her clit, the hard little pearl throbbing and swollen. Her legs shake, and I swear she's about to come from that one touch.

Without wasting any time, I grip her thighs and lift her up, pressing her against the door as she wraps her legs around my hips and digs her fingers into my shoulders. I look directly into her lust-filled eyes as I slam my cock inside her greedy little cunt.

Katya sucks in a breath and bites her lip to contain her scream. She comes as soon as I hit the end of her. I growl and hold myself deep inside her, feeling her orgasm from the inside out, wave after wave of ecstasy rippling from her core and dripping down my aching dick.

She buries her head in the side of my neck, panting and shaking and whimpering my name. It's more than I can take. I pull out of her pulsing, tight little pussy and push back inside, fucking her roughly, just like we both need.

"Valentino... oh fuck, Valentino... I-I-I'm..."

Holy shit. Is she...?

The goddess in my arms tangles her fingers in my hair and rips my head up, the sting shooting bliss straight to my cock, making it swell and stretch her out even more. Katya rests her sweaty forehead on mine, her chest heaving with each ragged breath as pained whimpers and grunts leave her mouth with each brutal thrust I give her.

"Come for me, princess," I growl.

My words unlock her orgasm, and Jesus, she comes so hard, shaking and sobbing out her release as her arms and legs squeeze me tightly. I grip her ass in both hands, holding her to me as I grind against her cunt and clit, keeping her right there, forcing her to feel it, feel me, feel every ounce of pleasure I'm giving her.

My balls are heavy with my pent-up orgasm, my dick throbbing and angry as fuck. But I want more. So much more. And I know exactly how I want it.

I set Katya down, her legs trembling much like the rest of her. She tilts her head up, peering at me through the fog of bliss surrounding her. I kiss her forehead, nose, and lips, allowing her to catch her breath.

And then I spin her around, pushing her forward so she has to brace herself with her hands on the door. I grip her cheeks, spreading her open for me so I can sink into her tight, wet little hole. With a feral roar, I snap my hips against her ass, stuffing her full of my thickness.

"S-s-so d-d-deep," Katya stutters out with a moan as her pussy contracts around me over and over.

I'm reduced to grunts and growls, tipping my head back and bouncing her off my dick. Every muscle in my body tenses and my balls draw up tight, my orgasm crawling down my spine and stealing the air from my lungs.

Sliding one arm beneath Katya's hips, I hold her still as I piston in and out of her. She claws at the door, then balls her hand up in a fist and pounds it against the wood as she succumbs to a final, vicious orgasm.

I slide my hand further down her body, rubbing her clit in furious circles as my other hand grabs a fistful of her silky black hair. She soaks my shaft with her cum and shudders in my arms. I bury my face between her neck and shoulder, breathing her in, feeling her shiver and pulse around me as I finally let go.

My orgasm barrels through me, clutching my muscles and making me shake uncontrollably as I come harder than I ever have. I shoot my release deep inside her still-throbbing core, each rope of cum forcing its way out in blissful, torturous waves.

It lasts forever, and yet it will never be enough. I know I'll want this woman wrapped around me as often as possible, chasing our pleasure and taking each other to heights unknown.

We both groan as I reluctantly pull out of her. I growl when I see our combined releases dripping down the insides of her thighs. I resist the urge to get on my knees and lick it up.

Katya leans against the door, pressing her forehead against the wood as she tries to control her breathing.

I smirk, knowing I gave her so many orgasms she can barely function. "Come here, baby," I say softly, holding out my hand.

Katya turns toward me, taking my hand and letting me gather her up in my arms.

"Love you so much," I whisper as I lift her and carry her to the couch.

"Love you, too," she mumbles, curling up on my chest once I sit down.

"I still can't believe you showed up at the Di Salvo compound to defend me," I tell her after a few moments of silence.

"I thought we already went over this, but I can give you a reminder if you need it." Katya lifts her head slightly, those golden eyes capturing mine as she smiles sweetly.

"I'm half-convinced I dreamt you up. There's no other explanation for why you want me."

My woman furrows her brow and flares her nostrils as she glares at me. "Valentino I-Don't-Know-Your-Middle-Name Rossi," she starts, her tone like that of a teacher scolding a disruptive child. "I don't want to hear you talk like that anymore. You're the most important person in my life, the only one who has ever given a damn about my well-being. You're selfless and fierce when it comes to protecting the things you love, and I take offense to your statement."

I can't help the smirk stretching across my face. She's so fucking adorable when she's all worked up like this, and over me, no less.

"I'm serious, mister!"

"I know you are, princess," I whisper, kissing her forehead and nose. "I'm still getting used to having someone care about me the way you do. It's humbling. I don't know what I did to deserve you, and I'm terrified I'm going to fuck it all up."

"I could say the same to you," she counters. "But instead of questioning our worth or worrying about the future, I say we just be thankful for what we've found. You're not going to fuck it up, Valentino."

"How do you know? What if I say something stupid or forget an important date or let the dishes pile up in the sink?"

"My love for you is bigger than all of that," she replies easily.

I grin, taking her lips in a tender kiss. "And my love is bigger than all of that as well," I whisper. "Thank you, Katya."

"For what?"

"For being you. For choosing me. For knowing how to soothe my dark places."

"Always," she murmurs, resting her forehead on mine.

"Always," I echo, cupping the side of her face to keep her close.

I soak up this moment with the love of my life, committing everything to memory. We'll be going to war soon, and knowing I have her waiting for me at home gives me the strength to do what I need to do. I will protect Katya and eliminate the threat of her family.

And then I'll come back and make sure Katya is mine forever.

CHAPTER TEN

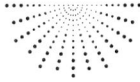

KATYA

"*H*ow many knives do you have?" I ask Valentino as he checks the magazine in his 9 mm handgun. "They're better for hand-to-hand combat."

Valentino pauses, looking at me with a raised eyebrow. "Is that so?" he asks with a grin.

"Yes," I tell him sternly, crossing my arms over my chest. "And stop smirking at me. You're heading into war, and I'm trying to give you some pointers."

His face softens slightly, those brown eyes finding mine and somehow imparting comfort and safety. We spent the rest of yesterday and last night in bed, with a few breaks for food and a shower. This morning, Romeo rounded up the troops and handed down orders. Valentino and the other men in the inner circle have been prepping all day, and now he's home to gather supplies before heading out to the Colombo warehouse.

"I've been doing this a long damn time, princess," he says, projecting confidence even though I see a hint of doubt in his deep brown eyes. No one else would notice, but I feel everything he's feeling.

"And I tackled your gun from your hands ten seconds after meeting you," I counter, lifting my chin and narrowing my eyes at the stupidly sexy man standing a few feet away from me.

Valentino smiles, then sets the gun down on the coffee table before holding his hand out to me. "Come here, Katya," he says soothingly.

I give him one last glare, then rest my hand in his open palm. He pulls me into his arms, pressing kisses to my temple, nose, cheek, and lips. Valentino circles his arms around my waist, drawing me closer as he rests his forehead on mine.

"I know you're worried," he starts, his voice washing over me like a cool breeze on a hot day. "But I promise you, I'll be right back here in your arms soon."

"But what if–"

"You can't think like that," Valentino whispers, smoothing his thumb over my cheek. "All the hypotheticals in the world won't make you feel better. Just trust that I have far too much to lose to do anything reckless. I have a job to do, and that's it."

"I could help," I plead for the tenth time today. "I can identify the major players in the family, help with attack strategy, or–"

"We've gone over this," he says, cutting me off. "I need you to stay here. Stay safe. I won't be able to concentrate if you're at risk."

I'm about to protest, but I know my words will fall on deaf ears. Taking a deep breath, I tilt my head up and close my eyes, trying to give voice to the sinking feeling I've had in the pit of my stomach all day.

"Something bad is going to happen," I whisper. "I can feel it."

"Something bad *is* going to happen. To the Colombos," he

says with a smirk.

I smack him on the shoulder. "I'm being serious. I love you, and I can't lose you. I won't." Tears burn the back of my eyes, but I don't let them fall.

Valentino's features turn serious, his hands coming up to cup my cheeks. "I love you too, Katya. I love you more with every day, every moment, every breath. You won't lose me. You have me forever, princess."

His lips find mine, and he leads us in a long, slow indulgent kiss, sweeping his tongue inside my mouth and making me forget about everything for a few blissful seconds. When we break apart, Valentino gathers up my hands in his, kissing my knuckles and then placing my hands on his chest, right over his heart.

"We'll be right back here, just like this, in a few hours." Brown eyes lock on mine, and I nod, wanting to believe him with every fiber of my being.

He gives me one last kiss, then steps back, slipping his gun into the inside of his jacket. Valentino strides to the door, and I wrap my arms around my torso, trying to hold myself together. He turns the handle, but right before he opens the door, Valentino looks at me over his shoulder.

"For the record, I have a knife strapped to my ankle, a switchblade in my pocket, brass knuckles, and two guns. Romeo will have bigger guns for us to use first, and we'll take every opportunity to snipe the enemy from a good distance before initiating hand-to-hand. Ideally, we just need to take out the guards and move the stockpile of weapons onto our trucks. They'll be distributed to our storage facilities, leaving the Colombos without the military power they are counting on to win this war."

Valentino holds my gaze as I nod, taking in his words. He's telling me the plan, trusting me with family secrets only the most loyal members have access to. It means more than he can comprehend. He's treating me as an equal, as someone worthy of trust.

"Thank you," I whisper.

He gives me a final nod, then steps outside, closing the door behind him.

Once again, I wait until I hear his car pull out of the driveway to jump into action. One day, my man will learn that I don't sit at home and wait very well. Until then, I'll have to keep surprising him.

I get dressed in a pair of black leggings and a black tank top, then I rummage through Valentino's closet until I find a dark long-sleeved t-shirt. Perfect.

Next, I pull open the bottom drawer of his dresser, just like I saw him do earlier this afternoon. Moving over the neatly folded shirts, I wedge my nail between the side of the wooden drawer and the false bottom, lifting up the piece of plywood to reveal a mini-armory.

There aren't any guns left, but I'm satisfied with a switchblade and a dagger with a curved blade. I tuck the smaller one into my bra and the larger one up my sleeve. I finish up my thief-in-the-night look by gathering my hair into a bun at the base of my neck, then check the time.

Nine-thirty on the dot. Perfect.

Slipping out the front door, I make my way down the driveway and out onto the street, walking a few blocks before turning left. There, at the end of the block, is the cab I ordered when Valentino was in the shower earlier today. I feel a little guilty for charging his card, but not guilty enough to call it off. Besides, I wouldn't have had to do that if Valentino let me go with him in the first place.

I hurriedly open the back door of the car and greet the driver, hoping he's not chatty. The man barely acknowledges me, so that's a plus. He rattles off the address I gave him in the initial call—a club that's not too far from the warehouse in question. I confirm and then melt into the seat, going over everything in my head.

I'm not sure what exactly I'm doing, only that I have to be there. All day, I've had a needling feeling that something is off. Something we're not thinking about or some angle we've miscalculated. I knew Valentino wouldn't let me tag along, but I can't sit back and do nothing. Not when the man I love could end up dead.

The cab winds through the dark streets of the city, punctuated by streetlights and neon signs. I don't realize I've spaced out until the car stops and the cabbie clears his throat. "You're not really dressed for the club," he grunts, his eyes meeting mine in the rearview mirror.

"How do you know I'm not a bouncer?" I counter. "Maybe I'm packing heat." This earns me an amused snort, which I take as a good sign.

I thank the driver and get out of the cab, meandering to the back of the line of club-goers waiting to get in. No one pays me any mind as I fade into the shadows along the old brick wall, then slip out of line and down an alleyway.

"Left, right, forward, forward, forward, left, forward, right," I whisper to myself on repeat. I studied the city streets on a map earlier today and found a route from the club to the warehouse using mostly back roads and alleys. It seemed simple enough at the time, but now I'm beginning to doubt my brilliant plan.

After what feels like hours, I'm about ready to give up and admit that I'm lost. But then I hear it. That voice. I'll never forget that raspy tenor or the way it makes me want to vomit.

Raffe D'Angelo, AKA the man who attacked me in my father's office.

"Hello? Bruno? You missed the last check-in." A moment

of silence, then, "Goddamn lazy twat. Never shoulda' been put on guard duty," he mumbles.

I press my back against the wall of the building and slink forward, closer to the voice I've learned to hate. Peering out from my hiding spot in the alley, I take note of Raffe standing about ten feet away, frowning at the walkie-talkie in his hand.

"Yo, Bruno must be high on the job again," Raffe shouts to someone off in the distance. "I'm headed to the north side to tear him a new one."

The man turns, and I get a good look at his face for the first time since he tried to force himself on me. Something in me snaps. All the years of neglect, abuse, helplessness, and anger expand in my chest, clouding my vision and making me strike without a second thought.

As soon as Raffe is within three feet of my hiding spot, I jump out, dagger in one hand, switchblade in the other. I slash that motherfucker's big jowls, smiling like a psycho when crimson pours out of his wound.

"What the fu–"

I stab Raffe in the gut with the dagger in my other hand, twisting the knife before shoving the bastard backward. He collapses on the ground with a satisfying thud, and I stand over him, pressing my foot down on his chest as I watch the life drain from his eyes. Good riddance.

Wrapping my hand around the handle of the dagger, I'm about to pull it out when a horrid screech fills the air.

"Katya! Katya what the fuck?"

I freeze in place, not sure if I should run or try to fight him. Trembling from head to toe, I look up to see my father sprinting in my direction.

"Are you involved with this raid? How the fuck… Where the fuck…?"

He's panting as he approaches, and I quickly withdraw the knife from Raffe's side, holding it out in front of me.

"Really?" my father scoffs. "You think you can kill me? You're *mine*, Katya. My daughter. And you *will* submit to my authority."

"N-no," I say in a shaky voice.

My father sneers at me, taking a step closer. "Fucking ungrateful bitch. You killed one contender for your hand in marriage, but I've got a dozen lined up. You will fulfill your destiny of expanding my empire, child. One way or another."

Something catches my attention from the corner of my eye, behind my father, and off to the right. Without moving, I flick my gaze in that direction, and relief hits me square in the chest. Valentino is here. He puts his finger to his lips, and I blink in acknowledgment. Valentino tips his chin up, motioning for me to lead my father past where he's squatting behind a few wooden pallets.

"I will die before submitting to you or helping you in any way," I spit out.

My father's eyes grow wide with fury, and I take the opportunity to throw the dagger in his direction before taking off toward Valentino.

"Fucking cunt," my dad growls, dodging the blade and stumbling back while I sprint away.

I pump my legs as fast as I can, pushing myself until my muscles scream and my lungs burn. I'm vaguely aware of my father lumbering behind me, but I keep running, leading him straight to Valentino.

"You can't escape me, I'm—"

"Nothing to her," Valentino roars, seconds before tackling my father to the ground. "You selfish, worthless, tiny man," he continues, placing his boot on my dad's throat as he stands once more.

I turn, keeping my distance from their fight but staying

close enough to jump in if necessary. My dad tries fighting back, but he's no match for Valentino. I watch as my man pulls out a gun, aiming it directly at my father's forehead. He looks at me, silently asking permission.

I nod once, squeezing my eyes shut when I hear the gun go off.

All hell breaks loose at that one shot. Shouts, more gunshots, engines revving, tires squealing, and complete pandemonium surrounds me. It's all too much, and right before I curl into a ball and cover myself for protection, Valentino is by my side.

"Surprise?" I say weakly, not sure how upset he is with me.

Valentino shakes his head, then scoops me up in his arms. "I suppose me telling you how dangerous this was won't have any bearing on you doing it again?"

"Probably not," I confirm, resting my head on his shoulder as he carries me back through the alley I was hiding in originally.

He lets out a small chuckle, then kisses my forehead. "Let's get you home, princess."

CHAPTER ELEVEN

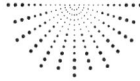

VALENTINO

*A*s soon as we make it back to my car, I get Katya settled in the passenger's seat and then peel out of the alley, heading straight to my home. Our home.

I grip the steering wheel and adjust in my seat, the adrenaline coursing through me and making it hard to sit still. Stealing a glance at Katya, I see she's staring out the window, her blank face reflected in the glass. She's shaking, her breaths fast and shallow.

Jesus, when I heard Marco Colombo scream Katya's name, my mind went blank. Nothing else mattered except getting to my woman. Everything had been going smoothly until one of the dead guard's walkie-talkies went off. We thought we took out everyone watching over the weapons stockpile, but apparently not. I was checking the perimeter for anyone we missed when Marco screamed.

There's no way I could have taken on the mob boss and his goon on my own, but thanks to Katya, I only had to handle her father. Even then, she led him right to me. I hate that she put herself at risk, again, might I add, but she wouldn't be the woman I fell in love with if she didn't fight tooth and nail to survive.

"Are you going to yell at me?" Katya asks.

I look over at her once more, those golden eyes finally resting on mine instead of out the window.

"No, baby. I should have known better than to tell you what to do."

My girl smiles at me, her hand finding mine on the center console. She weaves her fingers through mine, squeezing life back into every part of me.

We pull into the driveway of our home, and I waste no time bundling Katya up in my arms and carrying her inside.

"I can walk, you know," she tells me, even as she snuggles further into my embrace.

"This isn't for your benefit," I tell her. She gives me an adorably confused look, so I clarify. "I need you this close, Katya. I need to know you're here and we both made it out alive."

This makes Katya pop her head up from where she was resting it. "Oh my god, do we need to go back? We just left everyone there, and–"

"We're good, baby," I assure her as I make my way upstairs and into the bathroom. "We were almost done, and besides, you and I took out the big Boss. They can handle the clean-up."

"Are you sure?"

"I swear you almost look disappointed," I say, setting my woman down. Katya shrugs, which makes me smile, despite the crazy evening we've had. "Would you feel better if I gave him a call? I shot him a text right after…"

"Shooting my father?" Katya finishes for me.

I nod, still unsure of her feelings about everything. Yes, she gave me permission to end that piece of shit's life, but that doesn't mean she's not grieving.

"It's okay to say it," she whispers. "He deserved a lot worse."

I cup my hand around the back of her neck and pull her closer, pressing a kiss to the top of her head. "You're so strong," I murmur, kissing her one last time before stepping back. "You go ahead and get the water going while I call Romeo. Then I'll join you."

Katya nods, and I pull out my phone, dialing Romeo's number as I step out of the bathroom.

"Valentino," he answers, slightly out of breath. "It's over. Did you and Katya get home safe?"

"Yes, Boss. I wanted to check in. Well, Katya wanted me to check in."

Romeo chuckles. "I knew I was going to like her."

"So, what's the update? Did we lose any men?"

"Thankfully, no. We had already loaded up three of the four semis when Marco shouted for Katya. Is it true she killed Raffe D'Angelo? Or is Armando making shit up?"

"It's true," I confirm, pride welling up in my chest. "He was the prick who assaulted her. She got her revenge."

"Good," Romeo grunts before changing course. "We had snipers picking off the remnants of guards as the rest of us filled up the final semi. The Colombos have no armory and no leader. It will take years to rebuild and longer to retaliate."

"That's what I like to hear."

"You and me both. Now, go spend some time with your woman. I'll be indisposed for the next twenty-four hours, but we'll have a meeting after that."

"Thanks, Boss," I say with a chuckle. I'm sure Armando and Dante are spending the evening with their women as well.

Hanging up the phone, I toss it onto the kitchen table and then sprint upstairs to my Katya. The bathroom is practically a sauna, and I undress as quickly as possible, needing to see, touch, and feel everything about her.

When I pull back the curtain, I'm greeted with the sight of my precious, breathtaking woman dripping with water and surrounded by steam. She turns, holding her hand out for me. I take it, stepping inside our own little sanctuary of peace from the outside world.

"I can't believe you showed up tonight," I tell her as I smooth my hands over her curves.

"Really? It's kind of my signature move at this point," she teases.

I narrow my eyes at her, then nip the tip of her nose, making her giggle.

"I still can't comprehend why you'd put yourself in danger for me."

Katya's features grow serious, her magical eyes locked onto mine. "I love you, Valentino. Can't that be enough?"

"Yes," I choke out, cupping the sides of her neck with my hands. I brush my thumbs over her flushed cheeks, marveling at how soft she is. "I love you, Katya. More than I knew I was capable of."

I pull her closer, fusing our lips together as I tangle my fingers in her hair. My woman gives as much as she takes, her hands sliding up my back only to claw their way down.

When we break apart, Katya leans into me, resting her forehead on my chest. I keep her steady as I pour some body wash into my palm and slide my soapy hands all over her body. I massage Katya's sore muscles and take time to gently clean every inch of my fierce warrior goddess.

Katya returns the favor, soaping me up and running her hands up and down my torso, back, and legs. She trails kisses across my chest, and I tip my head back, closing my eyes and soaking up her gentle touches and sweet kisses.

"You feel incredible," I whisper, combing my fingers through her wet hair as she lavishes attention on me.

Katya takes a step back, and I tilt my head down, pouting at her. She grins, a mischievous glint in her golden eyes.

"I bet I can make you feel even better," she murmurs, biting her bottom lip.

Fuck me, how can I say no to that?

CHAPTER TWELVE

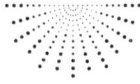

KATYA

*W*e're a flurry of hands and lips and sloppy kisses as we make our way from the shower to the bed. The back of my knees hit the mattress, but Valentino grips my hips, not letting me fall backward. He breaks our kiss and trails his lips down my neck, sucking on my pulse point, my collarbone, lower, lower, until he's licking my nipples.

I arch my back, thrusting my breasts into his face, needing more of whatever he's willing to give me. Valentino grunts in approval, sucking on one breast while kneading the other in his massive hand. I rub up against him, feeling his hot, hard erection graze my center. We both groan at the contact. Valentino grinds into me and sucks my tits, working me over and hurtling my already amped-up body toward an orgasm.

I feel his teeth and tongue everywhere, even though he's only playing with my nipples. Each stroke and teasing bite echoes throughout my body and lands a devastating blow to my clit.

"V-Valentino, it's… I'm…"

He glides his thickness through my folds, holding me by my hips while he continues to worship my breasts. The head of his cock taps my clit just as he bites down on my nipple, and my pussy gushes for him. I hold my breath, waiting for my climax to hit, even though I don't want this to end yet.

The next thing I know, I'm falling backward, my climax and frustration mounting with no means of release.

"Valentino!" I growl in irritation. I can't focus on anything else except the ache between my thighs and my trembling muscles.

"Patience, princess," he purrs. Valentino is still standing, watching me squirm while fisting his massive cock. He glides his hand up and down in rough strokes. I'm mesmerized by the motion, so much so that I find the strength to sit up and grab a hold of him, mimicking what he's doing.

"Oh fuck, love, you feel so good," he groans.

I smile, finally feeling like I have the upper hand, so to speak. I lean forward and kiss the tip of his cock, grinning when it twitches.

"Christ," he hisses.

"My turn," I murmur in what I hope is a seductive voice.

It must work because he closes his eyes and tips his head back like he's lost to my touch. I lick the pearl of precum that leaks out of him, moaning at his salty, earthy flavor. Valentino wraps my hair around his fist and draws my head back so I'm looking right at him.

"You want to suck my cock, dirty girl?" he grits out.

I nod my head as much as I can and dart my tongue out, flicking it against his throbbing dick.

Valentino clenches his jaw and narrows his eyes at me like he's considering something. Then, he nods once and pushes me back onto the bed, crawling up next to me and settling on his back. "You can wrap those pretty little lips around me, love, but I need to taste you while you do."

"Oh. Um… how?" I know my face is flushed at my stupid question. I want to do everything with him, but I don't want to disappoint him with my inexperience.

One look in his molten eyes, however, puts all doubts and insecurities to rest.

"I'm going to love teaching you all the ways your sexy fucking body can feel pleasure," he growls. "Now turn around and straddle my face, princess. Ride me while you suck me off."

His filthy words spark the fire that never went out deep in my core. I scramble to get into position, then hesitate as a wave of vulnerability hits me square in the chest. I feel so much more exposed like this.

Valentino doesn't let me get stuck in my head for long. He grips my hips and pulls me down, sucking on my pussy and making me cry out. He growls and digs his fingers into my flesh while eating me out in sloppy strokes.

I focus on his massive cock once more, licking and kissing down his shaft before opening my mouth and seeing how much of him I can fit inside.

"Holy shit," he barks out, tearing his mouth from my cunt. "That's it, love, that's so fucking it."

I moan at his approval, taking more of him and sucking him down over and over. I reach out and cup his balls, surprised at how hot and heavy he feels in my hand. Valentino makes a tortured sound in the back of his throat and sucks on my clit, hard, before scraping his teeth against the pulsing little button.

I pop off his dick and drag air into my burning lungs. I rest my forehead on his thigh, trying to catch my breath and steady myself. My entire body trembles, my muscles tense, my pussy throbbing and soaking Valentino's face as he licks me over and over.

He continues sucking on my clit and circles my entrance

with the pad of his thumb before pressing it inside. I slap the mattress with one hand, then ball up my fist, clenching the sheet and twisting it around my fingers.

"V-Valentino…" I whimper as my hips start to buck. I can't stop. I need more. Need him to put me out of my misery.

He hums and shakes his head back and forth, nearly making me collapse. I widen my legs and press my convulsing cunt down on his mouth, not even caring how wanton and slutty that makes me. He did this to me. He drove me to the brink of insanity.

It's right there, so close to the surface I can taste it. My long-awaited orgasm claws at my insides the way I'm clawing at the bed, desperate with the need for release.

"Off," Valentino growls, pushing me off him and to the side. I land on my back with my legs spread out. Tension wraps itself around my body and pulls every muscle tighter, tighter, tighter, squeezing the air out of my lungs but never letting me find relief.

"No!" I whimper. The need to come is so painful I feel tears burning the back of my eyes. "Please, please, please…"

Valentino sits up and grabs my hand, guiding it over my quivering pussy lips. He drags my fingers through my soaking slit, making me suck in air when I touch my clit. He grunts and uses my hand to rub furious circles over my swollen bundle of nerves.

I can't concentrate on anything other than how my body is shrinking in on itself, becoming a tight, compact ball of pressure so dense I feel like I might implode and cease to exist. I draw in a huge breath and feel my heart thud against my ribcage once, twice, three times, and then…

Every ounce of tension releases as my body expands and contracts in waves of shuddering bliss. I sob out my orgasm and try to escape from the intensity of it all, but Valentino doesn't let me. He holds my hand down on my clit and continues to rub up and down, side to side, and then in slow circles.

"Again. Make yourself come again, Katya."

"Wh-what?" I stutter, confused by his words. I can't focus on anything except the scream caught in my throat and the unbelievable pressure building swiftly in the pit of my stomach.

I don't understand how it's even possible to be at the peak of one orgasm while another is barreling toward the surface, but when it hits, all the air drains from my lungs as I let out a guttural scream.

"Jesus," Valentino mutters, pressing my fingers against my clit, keeping me right there, forcing my orgasm to reach every empty space, every muscle, every cell before it finally crests and starts to fade.

Valentino helps me turn around so my head is next to his and we're on our sides, facing each other. He traces his fingertips over the curve of my hip and the dip in my waist, back and forth, while never breaking eye contact.

I sigh contentedly, then remember I left my man unsatisfied. I had the most incredible climax, but he never came. I was too wrapped up in what he was doing to me to finish him off. Reaching out, I wrap my hand around his rock-hard shaft, making him inhale sharply and dig his fingers into my hip.

"I want to give you what you just gave me," I whisper, gently pushing on his chest with my free hand so he's lying on his back.

"Katya," he groans. "You give me everything by existing,"

I smile while I climb up his massive, muscled body, straddling him and running my hands up and down his torso. I start out with teasing touches, tracing the contours of his abs, pecs, and biceps. His muscles flex everywhere I touch, his skin heating as my pussy starts to pulse. He grunts when I score his flesh with my nails and rock against him, gliding my cunt up and down his thick dick.

"What if I want to give you more? What if I want more from you?" I bite my bottom lip and lift myself up on my knees, nestling his tip inside of my dripping opening.

"Fuck, take it, dirty girl. Take what you need. Feed that greedy pussy my cock until you come all over me."

My core clenches at his obscene words, making me tremble and suck in a breath. He can be filthy and brutal but also unbelievably sweet and tender.

Slowly, I ease my way down, feeling every inch of him invade me and fill me up. I know he feels it as his hands rest on my hips, holding me in place when I'm finally fully seated on him.

"Love being with you like this, Katya," he whispers, closing his eyes and breathing in deeply.

My pussy tightens around him as if agreeing with his statement. Valentino flexes his hips, wedging his cock deeper inside of me and making us both cry out. I grab his hands from where they are holding my hips and slide them up my body, placing them over my breasts. He takes the hint and squeezes my soft flesh, pinching my nipples.

I wrap my fingers around his wrists and grip him tightly, using his strength as leverage to buck my hips and grind down on him, testing to see what feels good for both of us. I angle my hips, hitting that spot inside me that drives me straight to the edge. I know it feels good for him when he squeezes my breasts roughly and growls.

Lifting myself up slightly, I drop down on him, hitting that same spot. I bounce on his cock, working us both up until we're sweating and shaking. I let go of his wrists and tangle my fingers in my hair, putting myself on display for my man. He makes me feel seen and loved and so desired. It makes me want to show myself off to him for his pleasure and mine.

"So fucking beautiful. So fucking mine," he growls, sliding his hands down my back to grip my ass.

He squeezes and separates my cheeks while thrusting his hips, fucking up into me so hard I fall forward. I catch myself on my hands, one on either side of his head.

"Valentino," I moan as he lifts my ass and then shoves me back down on his cock. He's so thick, so freaking long and hard, stretching me painfully, deliciously with each stroke.

My lips meet his in a frantic kiss, his teeth clashing, tongues tangling, breaths choppy and uneven as we get lost in our own rhythm. I snap my hips against his and bury my face into the side of his neck, unable to hold the weight of my head as a deep, drugging pleasure blankets and burns through me, destroying me in the best way possible.

"That's it, love," he groans. "So good, baby. So fucking good."

He slides one hand up my back and fists my hair, pulling my head up and holding it in place while he devours me. Each time he hits the end of me, sparks erupt and singe my nerves. My body feels heavy, swollen, and sensitive, but my head feels like it might float away on a cloud of bliss.

I tear my mouth from his, gulping down air while he fucks up into me in short, quick bursts. I match his movements as he spears me with his dick, over and over, breaking me apart one thrust at a time.

"Goddamn, look at us. Look at how well your tight little pussy takes my big cock."

I tilt my head down, looking between us. A wave of juices pours out of me, covering his dick. I whimper, loving the sight of him splitting me open.

"I can't hold on," I whisper, finally looking up at him.

Valentino's eyes are black with lust and the need for release. "I-I can't... I can't..."

Something inside me snaps and I lift my hips and slam my cunt down on him, grinding and swiveling my hips, fucking him desperately, racing toward my end. I can't stop. My body won't let me. My hips refuse to slow down.

I hold myself up with one hand and weave the fingers of my other hand in Valentino's hair, gripping it and forcefully yanking his head up so I can kiss him. His body responds to my manic, all-consuming, obsessive need to fuck hard and fast.

I cling to him as tightly as he's clinging to me, our bodies fusing together, grinding, rubbing, causing sweet, white-hot friction to spark a fire that blazes through us both.

"Fuck, fuck, fuck, little girl, need you to come for me. Need it, need, fuck, please..." he half groans, half growls.

Hearing this mountain of a man beg for me has my heart rattling around in my ribcage as lava floods my veins. I need to come so bad it scares me. I thought my last orgasm was the peak of pleasure, but the inferno threatening to swallow me whole is so much more intense. Flames lap at my nerves, and liquid heat courses through me, filling me up, then leaking out of my convulsing pussy.

"Let go, Katya. I'm here. I've got you," Valentino reassures me.

I make some undignified sound, then hold my breath, bracing myself for whatever lies on the other side of my release.

Valentino bites my shoulder and hits the very end of me in one brutal thrust. Flames engulf my body, burning me up from the inside out as I come, crying out his name. Tears well up and spill out of my eyes while sweat drips down my skin.

It's too much, yet not enough. I come again, but the ache

doesn't go away. Instead, it expands, seizing my lungs and heart, taking control of my limbs as I tremble violently. Valentino holds me close, his hands roaming up and down my back, my ass, my thighs, pressing my body impossibly closer to his like he wants to feel my orgasm with me.

My pleasure spikes again, this time unleashing a tidal wave inside of me. I'm embarrassed by how wet I am, but I can't stop. Every ounce of strength is wrung from my bones as heaving sobs wrack my body.

"Shit, you're squirting all over me. I feel it. Fuck, I feel it," he grunts.

I have no idea what he's talking about, but I don't have time to dwell on it. Valentino holds me still as he erupts inside of me. I feel his orgasm work its way through his body as he shudders against me. Thick ribbons of cum fill me up and spill out, joining my own release as it drips down my thighs and pools on the bed.

I don't know how long we're both suspended in our combined ecstasy, but when I finally come back into my body, I'm curled up into Valentino's side, my cheek pressed against his chest, right over his heart. I hear it thundering, his erratic heartbeat matching mine.

"Are you okay?" Valentino murmurs, placing a sweet kiss on the crown of my head.

"I'm perfect," I breathe out. "Blissful. Peaceful. Worn out." I lift my head, grinning at Valentino.

"You're definitely perfect," he says, his deep brown eyes peering down to the very depths of me. "And mine."

"Yours," I sigh contentedly. "Forever."

EPILOGUE

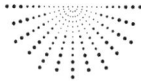

VALENTINO

"*H*appy birthday to you," everyone sings off-key, much to the delight of our seven-year-old daughter, Kaylee.

She rests her elbows on the table, clasping her little hands together as she looks around at her friends and family. Kaylee has her mother's golden eyes and strong spirit, which means she gets away with pretty much everything.

When the crowd finishes up their song, Kaylee's eyes grow wide as she takes in the cake Katya made especially for her birthday. It's a marble chocolate and strawberry cake with strawberry filling and chocolate frosting. My wife went all out, and I love that she found something she's passionate about.

After I put a ring on her finger and made her my wife, I encouraged Katya to go to college or explore hobbies and interests she was never able to when she lived with her father. She was hesitant at first, and it broke my heart when she confessed she's never let herself dream of a future where she gets to decide what she wants.

With some guidance and support, however, my princess

dove headfirst into the culinary arts, focusing on desserts and pastries. She runs a catering business on the side that's growing with each passing year. I couldn't be prouder of her and all of her accomplishments.

Claps and cheers echo around the dining room where we're hosting Kaylee's party, and then everyone scrambles for a piece of cake, knowing it will be incredible since Katya made it.

My phone buzzes in my pocket, and I'm about to shut it off when I see the name of a long-lost friend pop up on the screen.

Brewer Sullivan.

Stepping out into the kitchen for some privacy, I answer the call with more than a little curiosity. "Brewer? Is it really you?"

"Valentino," comes the gruff mountain man's voice. "Wasn't sure you'd pick up. Hell, I wasn't even sure this was still your number."

"It's been, what? Ten years? Twelve?" I muse.

"Therin about," he says, a slight country twang in his voice. "I hate to cut straight to the chase, but this is a time-sensitive matter."

"No problem," I reply. I'm not much for small talk anyway. "Is everything okay?"

"Is it too late to cash in that favor? You might not remember, but—"

"Of course, I remember. You saved my stupid ass on my first assignment."

I think back to the first time I met Brewer. He had just moved to New York City from his tiny mountain town in Nowhere, Idaho, and I was just starting out in the Di Salvo family, proving myself worthy.

I thought I'd get a gun from the Capo who gave me my first mission, but I found out real quick that weapons are earned. So there I was, barely nineteen, sent to deliver a package with no backup and no means of self-defense.

Long story short, I was tracked after making the hand-off and chased down by some crazy-ass motherfucker. Still don't know where he came from or what his problem was, but he got the jump on me before I even knew I was being chased. I could have handled one man on my own, but when three others showed up, I knew I was in bad shape.

That's when Brewer showed up. He grabbed one man by the back of his shirt and ripped him off of me, tossing him aside as if he weighed nothing more than a sack of flour. With that momentary distraction, I was able to scramble to my feet and help the stranger fight off the other bastards until they had had enough and ran away with their tails between their legs.

I had nothing to offer him at the time, so I promised him a favor to cash in once I was high enough in the ranks of the Di Salvo family. Looks like today is the day he's cashing it in.

"What do you need?" I ask after a moment of silence.

"There's a woman," he starts, making me smile. "More like an angel. A scared angel who has some secrets she thinks I can't handle."

"I can relate," I tell him, thinking of the first week with my Katya. We both had secrets and needed the safety of each other to confess them and heal.

"I need to know how to protect her. Can you look up information on people? I'm not sure what the scope of your influence is."

"Limitless."

Brewer chuckles. "Good. I'm going to need you to do some digging on her family and their business interests. And, uh, maybe you could gather some… other intel?"

"Something that could be used to blackmail someone, perhaps?"

"Exactly."

"Text me all the info you have and I'll run it through our networks. Might take a day or two."

"Thank you, Valentino. I mean it."

"I owe you more than looking up information. You saved my life."

"This is all I need. Keeping my angel safe is the most important thing to me."

"Well then how about I settle for an invite to the wedding?"

"Deal," Brewer grunts.

We say our goodbyes, and I head back into the dining room. My eyes are drawn to Katya, and I can't help but smile at how beautiful she is. Our three-year-old, Kira, is balanced on my wife's hip, sound asleep as sunlight from the bay window bathes both of them.

Katya returns my smile, weaving through the people to stand beside me.

"What are you thinking about?" she asks, gracing me with another smile.

"You, of course. It's always you."

Katya rolls her eyes, but I know she loves it. My woman went twenty years without hearing a single kind word, and it's my mission to make up for lost time.

I slip my hand into Katya's, weaving our fingers together as I lift her hand to my lips. "You're radiant today," I tell her, bending to kiss her temple.

"You always say that."

"It's always true," I counter.

My sweet girl blushes as she leans against me, resting her head on my shoulder. I wrap an arm around her waist and tuck her into my side, pressing a kiss to Kira's head and then Katya's. My heart is filled with pride and joy as I hold my wife and daughter and watch my other daughter obliterate her piece of cake the way only a child can.

"Love you," Katya sighs, her eyes fluttering closed.

"Love you more," I whisper.

Katya tips her head up, peeking one eye open. "Nope. Not possible. I'll fight you on this one, mister."

"I expect nothing less," I say with a chuckle.

My woman gives a satisfied nod before snuggling back into my embrace. I never thought I'd be this happy, never thought I deserved goodness in my life, but Katya changed everything.

I can't wait to spend the rest of my life showing her my gratitude.

* * *

THE END
Curious about Hawk & Savage Saints MC? Click here to find out more!

Want to know how Brewer's story ends? Get his book here!

Printed in Dunstable, United Kingdom